1

**With thanks to friends and family for support, editing and biscuits.**

To contact the author email styxworth@gmail.com

## Welcome to Styxworth

## Beginnings

Hi. My name's Dan. I used to have a normal quiet life. I enjoyed it. I was a cook in a small pub in a small town. In the evenings I would meet up with friends and we would do the things that friends do together. We would go to the cinema, we would go to parties and we would go for meals out. At one of the parties I met a guy called Pete. He was a friend of a friend. He was a tall skinny guy stood next to the stereo talking to a girl in a ratty green parka. My friend Chris introduced us. He told Pete that I liked to write the odd little story. And it's true. I did. I wrote the odd little tale here and there, usually in my notebook that I kept in my room at the pub.

Pete had a far away look, his clothes seemed old fashioned and his hair looked as if it had been cut by himself. As Chris introduced us his wandering gaze fell onto me. He looked me up and down and round about. When his eyes met mine I shivered. He seemed to look straight through me. "You like to write?" He asked me. I said that I did. "Well I have a tale to tell if you want to hear it."

"Don't we all?" I replied to him. His expression didn't change and his eyes shifted relentlessly about my face.

"This is a real story, I want it recorded and I think you could be the one to tell it to."

"How would you possibly know that?"

"I'm often led to decisions but this one I arrived at all by myself." He replied mysteriously. "Can we meet up tomorrow? Bring a tape recorder I want this told accurately."

"Um sure, when and where?" I stumbled.

"Tomorrow, your place, I don't want to be disturbed."

I nodded and gave him my address. "Come after seven, I finish work at six."

"Ok I will." And with that he turned his attention back to the girl he'd been talking to. She was thin, too thin, like she'd been ill recently. Her hair to was badly cut and her nails were chewed to the quick. Both looked slightly nervous and skittish.

The next day went much like any other. At six o'clock I handed the kitchen over to Dave the evening cook, we quickly signed the stock book and the rota and I left for the evening. In the small flat above the pub I pulled off my whites and took a quick shower. Dressed in fresh clothes I poured a glass

of beer from a can in the fridge and relaxed back in my seat. On the coffee

table was a small tape recorder and a fresh pack of batteries.

A few minutes before seven there was a knock on the door at the foot of

the stairs. I opened it and there stood Peter and the ragged looking girl from

the night before. I invited them both in and let them follow me up the narrow

stairs.

Seated upstairs, Pete in the chair next to the coffee table, me on a small

stool next to him and the girl on the floor next to the window. Pete took off his

thick coat and accepted a drink. She sat next to the window nervously

scanning the street.

"This isn't your ordinary tale that I'm going to tell tonight." He began.

"It involves my life and much more besides. What you hear tonight may seem

fantastic, but every word is true. It mostly concerns me but it could come to

affect us all." I shivered and pressed record on my tape player.

This is the tale he told me word for word. Nothing added nothing taken away.


**Holidays**.

Somewhere in the south of England lies the village of Styxworth. It's an unusual village in that it won't be found on a map and it won't be found by anyone that is looking for it.

Many people do go looking for it though. If you listen to the right people at the right time there are many stories about this strange place.

It is said to lie on the south coast of England, somewhere in Devon or Cornwall. Or maybe Dorset. No one is quite sure. The stories about the place, and there are many, are always told by people who haven't been. Sure enough they know of someone who has, or they know someone who knows someone who has been. Or they know of a man who knows a man who heard the story from a very reliable source. It's that kind of place.

But it is a real place. As real as the nose on my face. It just isn't tied to one place. It creeps up on the unwary traveler. You could be driving down an empty coastal road admiring the scenery when you come across a bend in the road, a dip to the left, quite normally, and then you find yourself driving through a village you hadn't noticed before. It all looks to be so quaint and oldy worldy you stop the car and get out for a walk about.

This is where the stories always start. The traveler entering the village, stopping the car and having a little walk about.

Our story starts here as well. But this isn't a second or third hand story. This one happens to be true. You see this story happened to me and my parents nearly 20 years ago.

My name is Peter Thwaites. My Dad was Chris and my Mum Jenny.


It had started out as any other holiday did. It was the first Saturday of the holiday. Dad had finished work at the office and Mum had finished at the bakery. He worked 9 to 5 at his office and Mum worked part time at the bakery in town.

School had finished  the day before at 3 and as the bell rang 200 kids spilled out onto the streets eager to start their 2 week holiday for Easter. We were to be spending a week at a small cottage in Cornwall near the beach. The weather was warm and we were all looking forward to the time away. I was also looking forward to spending time with my friend Colin, when we returned for the second week. We had made plans to go swimming and the cinema and maybe if we could sweet talk a parent a sleepover.

Life doesn't get much better for a nine year old boy than that.

Dad woke us all up early that Saturday bursting into my room singing about going on a summer holiday. Mum was behind him in her dressing gown laughing as he whirled about just wearing his pyjama bottoms. I got up smiling and laughing at him. As I carefully selected my holiday clothes from my drawers, Dad made breakfast, and he and Mum drank coffee. I had toast with jam and a glass of cold milk. The sun was just up as we put the cases in the car and put the bins out. Mum insisted on a last bout of cleaning and Dad poked fun at her asking who she was cleaning for....

We had a great day on the drive from our home in Lincolnshire to the south coast. At around midday we stopped at the services on the motorway for a break. Me and Dad went to the loo, and came out to meet Mum by the tourist information leaflets. Such attractions as a pencil museum and a clog factory were some of the delights that were on offer. We were joking about the kind of person that would go to these places when Dad noticed Mum had put a couple of leaflets in her handbag. He slapped his head in a melodramatic fashion and steered us into the food court. We left the services full of burger and high spirits. The motorway droned on beneath our tyres and Mum and Dad droned on together to the songs on the oldies radio station they liked to listen to.

Just past Exeter we hit what Dad liked to call the real roads. The roads that would lead us south to the Devon Coast. The end of the Jurassic Coast. The road tightened up and the hills got steeper. The pine woods grew thinner as we headed towards the English Riviera. The sun blazed in the blue sky and the wind rushed by our car window. Mum was driving and singing along to the radio. Her and Dad had just hit a kind of harmony when we crested the hill and saw the ocean in front of us. It was as smooth as glass, not a ripple or wave to mar its perfect form. The wind was taking a break today and the sun baked any other thoughts of movement from the day. Mum slowed and took the road to the right along the coast. With the sea to our left we motored along.

I opened the window to smell the sea. It smelled just like holidays and holidays meant freedom. Freedom from school, freedom from worries, and freedom from boredom for a whole week. The endless possibilities stretched out before me like the wiggly road in front of our small car.

With the scent of summer filling the back of the car I popped a straw into a juice box and was content with the world.

A little further on past bends and woods Dad called back we were going to take a toilet break and were on the look-out for a convenient spot. I thrilled at this as it normally meant entering the secret world of the pub. Dad would have half a lager, Mum would have a small white wine and I would have a bottle of coke with a bendy straw. If he was feeling particularly flush, then we might share a packet of crisps, split down the back so we could all dig in.

I loved the dim light inside these country pubs and the various smells, fried food and spilt beer mostly.

A sign pointed to a small road on the left, and Mum turned off the main road slowing as he entered the tight windy road. The sides of the road were steeply banked and gnarled with the roots of the trees that enclosed the road making it into a green shadowy tunnel.

"It's like driving into a Hobbit town down here isn't Pete?" Said Dad from the front, Mum concentrating on the tight twisty road.

"Do you think it could be the start of an adventure?" I asked.

"As long as I can have a wee first I don't mind" he replied.

We came out of the leafy tunnel via a tight left hand corner, and we drove slowly into a little village on the banks of a large river. The houses and streets were built onto the side of the hill which led down to the river, and on the other side the same was true. They were little houses and tight cobbled streets. A plume of smoke from one house curled gently into the sky. All of the houses were painted different colours and in various states of repair. The main road through the village led to the river where a ferry was chained up not moving on the river's edge. Down on the river front was a small car park where Mum pulled in.

"Go and see how much it is Pete."

I ran up to the ticket machine, my trainers slapping the hot cobbles. Reading the sign I ran back and got 50p from Dad. I returned panting with a ticket clamped in my sweaty hand.

We wandered down the line of houses and shops on the river front basking in the sun.

"Not a cloud in the sky, not even aeroplane trails," said Mum.

"You're right there's nothing up there at all" replied Dad. He squinted down the street looking for the tell tale sign for a pub. Spotting one he took Mums hand and quickened his pace up the street.

Standing outside the pub we looked up at the sign.

"What do you reckon Pete, do you want to go and swill grog in the Ferryman?"

Something about the dark hooded figure on the sign didn't sit right with me but I was hot thirsty and needed the loo.

"Sure Dad. What's grog?" I asked

"It's what all good pirates drink." Dad's pirate voice was pretty good.

He leaned round the open door and asked the barman if it was OK if I came in for a drink.

A muffled reply came then Dad looked back grinning saying, "Come aboard ship mates!"

Inside the bar was cool and dim, the windows thick with grime turned the sunshine a sickly yellow. Two or three small  flys turned lazy loops around the tray under the beer tap. A small TV in one corner showed a horse race and two aged men watched it with grim concentration.

Dad stood at the bar ordering the drinks while me and Mum took a table.

After we've visited the toilet we sat together enjoying the lazy atmosphere, the way the diffused sunlight coming through the window made the tired brass fittings shine. The unrushed, unhurried air spoke of days stretched out to breaking point filled with nothing but leisure. I sipped my coke through a straw and nibbled a crisp.

"How much further have we got to go dad?" I asked.

"About an hour or so, depends on how fast yer Mum drives I suppose!" He grinned as Mum swatted at him, the lazy slap glancing off his arm.

"So you're not sticking about?" The barman asked from his spot at the bar.

"No we're off down the coast to a small cottage in Cornwall. Just stopped off for a comfort break and to take in the scenery" said Dad.

"Shame, tis a place that people say once you visit you can't leave." He smiled a strange smile and sloped off to serve one of the old boys watching the small grimy TV in the corner.

Mum picked the glasses up in one hand and placed them lightly on the bar. "Thank you" she called as we stepped into the bright mid afternoon light. The barman and the old boy at the bar waved a lazy hand in return as the door swung shut behind us.

Slowly we wandered back towards the car. The streets seemed quiet and there were only a few people on the sandy beach next to the river. A young girl about my age in a short sleeved t shirt and scuffed jeans caught my eye as she was looking right at us, arm raised to her forehead to block out the sun.

Back in the car park Dad unlocked the car and opened the door. A wall of heat fell out. Mum opened the other door and we stood next to the car letting the heat fall away from the interior of the car. Dad pulled the seat forward and I clambered into the back. I pulled my seat belt on and clicked it into place. Mum did the same, winding the window down as she pulled the door to. Dad slumped into the drivers seat, moving the seat back after Mum

had been driving.

He pushed the key into the ignition, turned it, and, nothing. Not even a click.

He frowned, took the key out turned it over and tried again. Not even a click.

Frowning he tried again. Nothing.

He checked the lights to see if they had been left on, exchanged a worried

glance with Mum and tried again.

The car was dead.


**The dead car.**


After a few hurried words with Mum they came up with a plan of action.

He would try and find a garage or mechanic and we would go for a walk.

"Probably just a dead battery." He said with a forced smile.

Mum took my hand and we walked off down towards the bank of the river.

The river was wide and looked sluggish in the bright light of the afternoon.

The banks were sandy and I got the impression we weren't far from the sea.

There was an ice cream van on the road across from some steps that led down

to the beach.

"Fancy an ice cream Pete?"

"Sure, can I have a 99?"

Mum smiled and nodded and we headed over to the van. As Mum placed the order and the man got our cones ready I looked around. The girl I'd seen outside the pub stood looking at me. She had long tangled brown hair and was very tanned, as if she had been outside a lot. She had her hand over her eyes, shading them from the sun as if to see me better. Somehow I knew she wasn't staring at the van behind me.

"Here you go Pete." Said Mum as she handed me my ice cream. I took it and looked back but the girl had gone.

"Come and sit on this bench while you finish your cone, I know what you're like and I don't want you dropping it. I ain't buying you another."

So we sat in the sunshine eating ice cream, the only sounds were the ice cream van and the smacking of our lips. I enjoyed my ice cream, I had developed a special technique to stop it dripping down my arm, you put your tongue out and kept the cone turning against it to prevent dripping. But sure enough by the time I had crunched the last of the cone Mum had to come to the rescue with a wet wipe.

After cleaning up we took a stroll over to the steps leading down to the sandy beach. The heat haze made the other side of the river look mysterious and dream like. There was a small ferry moored up the river at a small dock.

On the other side was another  although  they didn't seem to be doing much business today. I couldn't make out a pilot on either boat.

We walked with our back to the ferry heading downstream the town to our left. We passed the front of the pub and kept walking down. I was on the look-out for flat stones as I had learnt how to skim stones the previous summer.

We had gone to visit my grandparents who had a little cottage near a lake. The lake was in a hollow of hills and a perfect circle. Me and Grandad had spent many hours on the small pebble beach trying to make stones skip and dance across the water. My best had been six bounces and I was keen to better this on this trip.

Sadly this beach seemed to mostly be made of sand but the occasional pebble showed itself.

The houses were starting to thin on our left so we turned round and began a slow walk back up the beach.

"Let's go and see how Dad is getting on with the car shall we?" Said Mum. She seemed keen to be off.

"It's a little too quiet here, I'm not sure I like it." She said as we plodded back towards the ice cream van and the dead car.

Back at the car Dad was nowhere to be seen. We sat on the wall of the car park and waited.

"The last thing we want is to be looking for him while he's looking for us. That way we'll be here forever" she laughed. Her eyes darted up the street and back again. She looked at her watch and muttered "Now where can that man be?"

Five minutes later Dad was back. He didn't look happy.

"The local garage is shut until Monday" he told Mum. "I've spoken to the landlord of the pub, he's going to bring his car round with some jump leads to see if he can get us going. If not he does do rooms."

"Great, I thought that in an hour or so we would be unpacking the car at our cottage not checking in to a pub." She snapped.

"I know but there is nothing we can do, all we can hope is that the jump leads work."

And with that a car turned into the car park and flashed his lights. Dad waved and the landlord from the pub drove over to us and got out.

"Right pop the bonnet and let's see if we can get you on your way." Dad opened the bonnet and propped it up, the land lord did the same. He fetched some leads from his boot and clipped them onto his battery. I went and stood next to Dad as I'd never seen this done before.

"Hang back a little there Petey. Don't want you hurt if this goes wrong."

He clipped the leads on with a little spark that made me jump. The land lord revved his engine and Dad got into our car. He turned the key and again there was nothing, no cough, no splutter, no click.

"Leave her a minute or two" the land lord called. "See if we can't push some life into her."

The land lord continued to rev his engine as Dad leaned on his window talking softly to him.

"Right, give her another try, let's see if she's gonna go."

Again Dad tried and again nothing. Mum looked frustrated and Dad was a little pale.

He unhooked the leads and thanked the land lord.

"Do you want me to get Trudy to make up the family room?" He asked.

Dad nodded. "We'll grab our bags and come in a minute."

The land lord closed his bonnet and drove back around the corner.

"Right grab your bag Petey looks like we're going to be staying here a couple of days."

"How much is this going to cost?" Mum asked Dad.

"The car? I won't know til Monday. The room? He didn't say but I can't imagine it being much and we're not going to sleep in the car."

We walked slowly back to the pub. When we got there the landlord greeted us and led us upstairs to the room. As we reached the top of the stairs a door was pushed open. A large cheery looking woman stepped into the hall.

"Ah, you must be our guests," she beamed. "Come in, come in. Bob told me about your car so you relax until you get it fixed. And who might you be young master?" She asked smiling down at me.

"I'm Peter."I replied.

"Well Peter when you get all unpacked you and your Mum and Dad will have to have a good old explore of the village. There's more to Styxworth than meets the eye sometimes."

She gave me a large wink and bustled us into the room before sweeping out and closing the door behind her.

"Well let's get comfy then, we'll unpack and go out on the town shall we?" Said Dad. "We are still on holiday after all."

## The Village

We stepped from the pub into the cool afternoon air. Evening was fast approaching. Before we left the room we had opened all of the windows. The room, while clean had the air of being unoccupied for a long time. We walked down to the bank of the river to the beach and walked down to the waters edge. I was keen to show Dad how I was improving at skimming stones.

"Find some good flat stones then Petey. Down at the waters edge should be a good place, just watch to not get your feet wet."

I nodded and skipped down to the side of the slow moving river. Looking back up towards the village you could see the ferry was still moored at the dock not moving. I turned back to my task of finding some good skimming stones.

With a pocket full and a bunch more clutched in my hand I looked round for Mum and Dad. They had walked a bit further down the beach. As I headed toward them I saw the same girl from earlier crouched at the top of the bank looking at me. She regarded me with no fear or shame. I waved and she waved back, and with that stood and with a flick of her hair walked back to the village.

Me and Dad had a good time skimming the stones across the river. His best was a five bounce and mine was a four, Mum didn't want to take part. We climbed the bank of the river and walked back towards the village on the small road leading up to it from the south. The sun was getting lower in the sky turning the world into shades of orange and gold. The houses stacked up the hill became silhouettes and the air stood still. We walked past a few closed shops and the iron gates in front of the church. As we turned down into the road to the front of the pub the same girl was there leaning against a wall.

Cheap sunglasses held her mane of hair back from her face and her tan skin glowed in the evening light. She flashed a smile of pearly white teeth at me waved and ran off.

"Friend of yours?" My Dad asked teasing me with a nudge in the side.

"Dunno just keep seeing her about." I replied feeling lightly embarrassed.

Dad pushed open the door to the Ferryman and we went inside for tea.

The next day announced itself early with sun pouring through the curtains. Taking the opportunity I took a book from my bag and started to read for a bit while Mum and Dad were still asleep.

When they awoke an hour or so later we all got washed and dressed. There was a knock at the door, Dad answered and Trudy popped in.

"Morning morning, would you all be liking a bit of breakfast?" We nodded that we would. "Full English all round then?" Again we nodded. "See you in the bar then. Bob's just gone to fetch some papers."

We trooped down to the bar and took a seat at a table laid for breakfast. Presently Trudy reappeared with a huge tray. She set down three large plates bearing sausages, bacon, eggs, black pudding, beans and a mushroom each. She returned with a plate of toast and set it down. We all tucked in as a jug of fresh orange juice was plopped on the table.

When Trudy returned to the kitchen I slipped my mushroom over to Dad's plate. I've never liked them.

When we were finished we sat feeling a little stuffed after such a feast.

"So what is the plan of action for today?" asked Dad.

"Well it's Sunday so I don't think much will be open. We could go for a walk down the beach, I don't think the sea is far away." suggested Mum.

"Anything you want to do Pete?" asked Dad.

"I might want an ice cream later, but other than that I don't know. Skim some more stones maybe?"

"Then it's a plan. We go to the river, skim some stones and eat ice cream." said Dad.

We trooped back up to the room and put our trainers on. We cleaned our teeth and headed downstairs into the pub. Bob was behind the bar getting ready to open and Trudy was wiping down the tables.

"So what's the plan for today then guys?" Bob called over.

"Taking a walk down to the river to skim some stones and maybe find the sea, then we will try and fill Pete here with ice cream."

"Mind you don't go in the river, strong current, been known to carry people away. As for the sea you won't get past the headland I'm afraid. We're in a bit of a valley here. Sheltered you know"

"Oh well, two out of three ain't bad." Said Dad. "Are you doing tea tonight?"

"Of course, we put on a roast for lunch but tea is normal menu. If old Colin the fisherman pulls his finger out there may be some fresh fish to fry..." sighed Bob, "but I'm not holding my breath." He laughed and returned to polishing his brass taps.

We turned and headed out into the sleepy village.


We strolled through the empty streets, down towards the river. The ferry was docked up at the slip way still showing no signs of moving. Down at the rivers edge Dad looked at the water and said "I know it doesn't seem fast flowing but if Bob reckons there is a strong current you be careful not to go in, OK Pete."

"I will Dad, I've got my new trainers on and I don't want to get these wet. Mum would kill me."

He laughed and nodded. "True true Pete, now let's find us some skimmers."

We walked along turning over stones with our feet and looking for good flat stones. Once we had a good hand full each we turned to face the water and started to skim. I was getting a good three or maybe four bounces on each stone. Dad was getting more. I said it was because he's stronger, but he said it's to do with the spin he gives each stone. He showed me how as he throws each stone, he ran his finger along the length of it giving it extra spin.

We were down to our last stones, Mum called down to us to see if we were ready for some ice cream yet. Me and Dad nodded to her and agreed these would be our last ones.

"Let's give our best throw, remember to really spin 'em this time." said Dad.

I threw first and with the little splutter at the end I claimed a five bounce. Dad leaned back and gave his last one some welly. He turned to look up at Mum, when I am sure I saw a hand reach up out of the water and grab his stone.

"How many did I get Pete?" he asked.

"Uh I think four but I think something caught it!" I sputtered.

"Something caught it? Was it a fish or a mermaid?" said Dad laughing a little. "Too much time out in the sun and not enough ice cream I think."

I started to protest but stopped as he turned his back laughing.

We walked up the beach to where Mum stood. "I almost won the stone skimming but we think the man from Atlantis caught the last stone!" said Dad laughing as he spoke.

"Really, that's a stroke of bad luck Chris. Too much sun Pete? Must be ice cream time then."

But I knew what I had seen.

At the ice cream van we all chose our ice creams. As we sat licking round the ice cream to stop drips running down our hands, the girl I kept seeing walked down the road. Her mane of hair was held back with a length of brown hairy string and the cheap plastic sunglasses were perched on the edge of her nose. She looked at me over the top of them raised here eyebrows and said Hi. I said hi back, turned and looked at Mum and she nodded. "If you want to go and play feel free. Just meet me and your Dad back in the pub at five OK?"

 I nodded and walked over to the  girl."Hi" she said "My name is Bex. It's short for Rebecca but I hate that. I only get called it if I'm in trouble." She smiled at me flashing those white teeth at me.

"I'm Pete" I said. "Do you live here?" I asked.

"In Styxworth? Yup, been here since I can remember. C'mon lets go to the beach, if we go up river there's some private places we can play."

We walked off down the quiet streets towards the river. At the top of the hill the church bell rang in the time. It was one in the afternoon. We walked up the beach stones clicking beneath our feet, I picked up a few potential skimmers, "Bex, can you skim stones? I got up to five on my last go."

I pulled my arm back and went to throw. She caught my arm by the elbow and said "Best not to Pete. You don't want to annoy anything living in there."

I looked at her, "My Dads last throw I thought I saw a hand catch the stone. You don't mean....?"

I let the question hang in the air between us. She nodded and stopped walking. "Styxworth isn't like any other place you know. It's uh, different. But I can't show you. You have to see for yourself."

"Is that where we are going now?" I asked.

"Kind of, it's a cave but it has a weird vibe. I dunno, but I don't think anyone has been in it in years. The entrance is hidden but I know the way."

We walked on along the beach Bex leading the way. We approached the small hill at the end of the shingle. The bare earth led down into the water of the river. Behind a willow tree Bex pulled branches away revealing a small hole in the rock. She turned sideways and slipped inside. Such was her confidence I followed her in without a look back.

## The Cave

Inside the cave sparkled. It glowed as if lit from inside. Bex pointed out the hole in the ceiling. "The hole is on the water side of another willow tree. You can't see it unless you know what it is you are looking for. At this time of day the sun light hits the hole and illuminates the whole cave. I love it in here, it's my escape from the world, a place to hide."

I stared around at the sparkling rock, it was very smooth and what looked like flecks of gold embedded in the rock were the cause of the glittery light. "It's amazing, how did you find it?" I asked.

"I was being chased by a dog and I hid in the tree outside. As the dog got closer I moved round and through the branches, then I found this place. The dog didn't follow me in and it left soon after. After I came in it couldn't seem to see or smell me. It's odd but I like it."

"Why was a dog chasing you?" I asked.

"I don't know, it came running towards me when I was on the beach one day and it didn't look like it wanted to play, so I ran. Since that day I don't throw stones in the river."

She looked at me and flashed her smile, she took her sunglasses off and pushed them back through her mane of hair. "I like it here, I always feel safe, but it does have a weird vibe, don't you think?"

I reached out and ran my hand over the wall. It left a glowing line where my hand had been.

"Wow do that again!" She whispered.

"Eh, is that not normal?"

"No its never done that for me."

I reached out and pressed my hand against the wall. When I pulled it away a glowing hand print was left, slowly it faded away.

"Wow" we both said.

We spent the next ten minutes drawing shapes on the wall, a glowing gold flecked graffiti that faded as soon as I finished it.

"We should go soon, time moves differently when you're in here."

"Oh really, shame. Will you be about tomorrow? It's nice to spend time with kids my own age."

"Yes of course, shall we meet on the beach at twelve?"

"Yes sounds good. Dad is going to try to get the car fixed tomorrow so we can play all day if we like."

She smiled at me in a strange way then turned and led the way to the hole in the wall. I trailed my fingers along the wall leaving glowing contrails behind me.

Back out in the sunshine we pushed away the branches of the willow tree and walked up the beach to the road. The church bell in the distance started to chime. It rang out five times. Bex looked at me and nodded, grabbed my hand and ran off pulling me up the road towards the pub. We reached the door a few minutes later, she kissed my cheek and ran off laughing. Over her shoulder she called "til tomorrow Petey."

I waved and pushed the old wooden door to the pub open.

"Oh look Jen here he is, he's been kept out late by a woman!" Dad waved at me from the bar.

"Go and wash your hands. Do you want a coke?" asked Mum.

I grinned nodded and went through to the toilet and washed my hands.


We ate dinner that night in the bar. Old Colin hadn't pulled his finger out so there was no fresh fish but I had a chicken pie with chips and beans. Bob the barman laughed when I asked for some bread and butter to make the pie pastry into a sandwich. After dinner Dad stayed in the bar for a drink and me and Mum went upstairs. She asked me what I had been up to with my new friend.

"She's called Bex and she's really cool. We played down by the river, there's a tree at the other end and we raced sticks in the river."

"You were careful weren't you, you heard what Bob said about the river?"

"Yes Mum, Bex is local and knows all about it."

I don't know why I chose not to tell her about the cave but I felt that was between me and Bex. Our secret together gave us a bond and I quite liked that.

Mum seemed to be OK with that as she got into bed and opened her book. I turned over in bed and reflected on the day. From the hand in the river yesterday to the cave today, it had been an odd couple of days.

The next day dawned bright as the sunlight lasered through the gap in the curtains. Dad was snoring lightly so I took the time to read some of my book. I was looking forward to seeing Bex again and maybe going back to the cave.

Presently Dad and Mum woke up and we went downstairs for Breakfast. Trudy greeted us and we sat at the same table as yesterday. We sat and ate our substantial breakfast and over toast and marmalade Dad outlined what he hoped would happen today.

"Now hopefully the man from the garage is going to have a look at the car and it will be an easy fix. Then after it has been mended we can have a nice meal tonight and be on our way tomorrow morning. What have you got planned today Pete? Seeing your new girlfriend?"

I blushed a little and nodded. "We're meeting at midday." I mumbled.

"I'm going to have a pleasant day poking around the shops I think." said Mum.

"Well that's everyone sorted then, shall we meet back here at five again for tea?"

I nodded and Mum nodded as well. I had an hour before me and Bex were going to meet so I decided to take a walk with Mum up to the shops in the village.

Dad went to the bar to speak to Bob about contacting the local mechanic. As me and Mum walked out Bob looked to be giving some elaborate directions with much waving of his hairy arms. As Dad turned and started copying his directions it reminded me of a wildlife documentary we had watched about gorillas just the other night. I walked out of the pub chuckling to myself.

After what seemed like an age walking around the shops I heard the church bell ring a quarter to the hour. I looked at Mum and she nodded, kissed me on the cheek and said "Be careful by the river. I'll see you at five."

I turned and ran off down the street, my trainers barely touching the tarmac. I skidded to a halt at the road looked both ways and carried on to the beach. As I hit the beach I slowed to a walk as those stones could trip you easily. I could see a figure up by the willow tree. It was Bex, she was looking at the river but as I approached she turned and waved. I waved back and quickened my pace.

"Hey Pete, whaddya know Eskimo?" she called as I walked up.

"Eskimo?" I asked.

"I dunno, it rhymes, I've got loads of them. My Dad used to use them all the time."

"OK I get you. Like, see ya later alligator?"

"Yeah just like that. Whaddya heard lemon curd?"

I laughed and tried to think of one. "Um what's the deal spinning wheel?" I asked uncertainly.

"It's a start I suppose. So do you want to go into the cave again?"

"Sure I do. I wonder if I can make it glow again?"

"Let's see." She turned her back and went through the overhanging branches of the willow. She turned sideways and seemed to melt through the gap in the wall. I turned sideways to follow. I heard a startled OH from her and as I emerged into the cave I saw why.

**In the Cave**.

There in the middle of the cave sat a man. He was an old man with a long white beard.

He sat on the floor cross legged with his eyes shut and he seemed to be humming. Not a tune but a long resonating tone. All the walls of the cave seemed to glow in response to his hum, throbbing in a pale jaundice yellow as he drew breath and hummed on. At my own startled OH he stopped and looked up. The glow on the walls ceased and the only light was that that fell from the hole in the roof.

Slowly he opened his eyes and looked at us both. In a voice deep like distant thunder he spoke.

"The Guide has finally found her calling. Welcome to you both."

We both stood there dumbfounded unable to speak.

"I'm sure my presence comes as quite a shock to you both. There is nothing to fear though. I am from an ancient order of people sent to watch for answers in times of trouble in Styxworth. And you young sir," he fixed me with a steely gaze, "are the answer to our present predicament."

"Predicament?" I asked.

"There are things you need to know about Styxworth and this place before I can lead onto our predicament. I think the young lady knows or suspects some of these things already."

Bex looked at him her mouth hanging open a little.

"You called me a guide before, I'm not sure I know what this place is let alone anything else, how I can be a guide?"

"And yet you led him here to the cave. You may not yet know everything but destiny has led you to each other, and led you here. What can you tell me about Styxworth?" he asked.

"Um I'm not sure, only that it's not like anywhere I've been before. There are odd things here I can't understand."

I knew she was thinking about the dog that chased her but I was thinking about the hand in the river.

"Styxworth is an ancient place that is between worlds. The living cannot perceive it and the dead no longer need it. It is a place for restless souls. Some are on a journey and some are here for an eternity stuck between the plane of the living and the world of the dead."

"But we're on holiday." I said to him. "Our car broke down after we stopped here. The mechanic in town is trying to mend it today."

"Your car will never be mended. It is a thing of the living world not of Styxworth. You and your family are stuck in limbo for now."

"But we only stopped off for an ice cream...." I stuttered.

"There was a terrible accident, your car collided with a tractor that had broken down on a blind corner. The impact was swift and as your physical bodies fight for life in a hospital your souls have come here. Styxworth serves as a comfort to souls newly departed from their physical hosts."

"So you mean to say me and Mum and Dad are...." I couldn't finish the sentence.

"Not yet,but soon I fear it could be so. Because of the shock of the event, the truth is cushioned in this place. Soon you will come to realise. Your parents are about to find out that the car cannot be fixed. For the time being you will stay here until it comes time to cross the river. Or they may choose to stay in the village, to help others, like the owners of the pub. They will be the ones to break the news to your parents. They will give them the choice of a new life here or to continue on across the river."

I sat down hard on the cold floor of the cave. The shock hit me like a slap. "But what about Bex? Surely she's not...."

"Not yet." He fixed Bex with a gaze. Her smile had left her face and her bottom lip quivered a little.

"Her body lies in a hospital. Physically the doctors can find nothing wrong with her but she can't wake up. They have tried many things but she continues to exist in the realm between worlds. I believe that she has been here waiting for you. She is your guide and as long as you need her, here she remains."

"So your parents aren't here?" I asked her.

She shook her head. "I live up the hill at the back of the church. The vicar there takes care of me."

"Did you know all of this?" I asked.

"Only some, I was so upset when I woke up here. I woke up on the beach and couldn't find Mum or Dad. I was scared and alone. I walked through the streets crying but no one could touch me. Bob and Trudy at the Ferryman tried to help but I kept walking. It wasn't until I saw the church lit up that I decided to seek comfort there. I was confused and scared, the vicar took me in and gave me some food. He tried to explain it but I didn't really want to hear it. His talk of God and man did nothing to answer the questions I had. But over time I grew to accept my new circumstances."

I knew some of how she felt. Was I lucky both me and my parents were here? Was our life threatening condition a good one to share? What if one of us survived when would we meet again? What did all of this have to do with me?

I wanted to reach out and strike something, to hurt or be hurt. Anger and a deep sadness duelled within me. I shouted in frustration and leant against the rock wall of the cave. All at once the wall glowed a deep resonating gold colour and a calmness swept through me with the lightness of a dove. I felt destiny stretch her wings and settle them round me. I turned to the man with the beard and fixed him with a stare. "So what is it you want with me?"

"Within you lies a power that few possess. You see it when you touch the rock around you. I have studied the technique and form for years yet all I produce is a sickly weak glow. You arrive here for the first time and make the walls glow golden without a thought. The power is with you. We need that power here in Styxworth. Our realm is under attack from an insidious source, one we ancients cannot reach, all we can see are the symptoms. The ferryman will not sail his ferry to the other side. If this goes on for much longer the souls will overwhelm us and a catastrophe awaits. The problem is that we don't know where or how this plague has reached us."

His talk drained him, his tired eyes turned towards me.

"You think I can help?" I asked.

"I believe you to be the One , the Traveller. You have met your Guide and I am your Watcher. The circle is complete ."

"But I'm dead, as is my family. Why should I help you now?" I cried out to the bearded man.

"Because if you don't you and your family might be stuck in limbo forever. As the population increases here in Styxworth it will become a most unpleasant place. All of the scum of humanity will wash up here unable to move to the other side and corrupt its balance."

I felt sick to the pit of my stomach. "But why is it left to me, who am I to take on this quest?"

"You are the Traveller. You can move between the realms and bring about balance," he calmly said holding my gaze, "but first you need training in the manipulation of the power around us. But that will have to wait for tomorrow. I feel your parents are just getting some bad news. Until tomorrow Traveller. Until tomorrow......" His voice faded as the light from the walls dimmed.

"Wait, what do I call you? I can't just call you watcher."

"My name is Mehari. You may call me this. I will see you at this place tomorrow. The guide as well, your destinies are now intertwined." As the light dimmed he slipped back into the gloom until he disappeared completely.

I turned and pushed Bex aside as I felt for the exit. Everywhere my hands touched I left glowing hand prints. These illuminated my path out. Through the gap in the rock I fell, grateful for fresh air and clean sunlight. The willow branches stroked my face as I collapsed panting. Feeling the bile in my stomach rise I breathed deep to stop the vomit. Then a cooling hand on my sweaty brow brought me back from the brink. Bex was kneeling next to me, her cool palm on my brow.

"How could you not tell me?" I whispered.

"I didn't know how, I'm so sorry but there aren't any other children here. I knew you would find out sooner or later but I really wanted a friend. I wanted someone I could share my cave with. The strange thing is from the first moment I saw you I knew you were kinda the one. The vicar always told me that the realisation of the situation has to be handled carefully. If it's done too soon then the that person can cross over not prepared and their own guilt and fear can have horrible consequences."

"Really?" I asked confused.

"A soul not at rest can be condemned to wander the extent of their own guilt in a hell of their own making, only a soul at rest can live at peace in the afterlife. Or at least that's what the vicar told me." She cast her eyes down at the ground and held out her hand. "Friends?"

I didn't even hesitate, I took her hand and said "Of course we are. It would seem you are my Guide. Now I best get back to the pub. I think Mum and Dad could need me."

Back at the pub Mum and Dad were sat at a table with Bob the barman having a very in depth conversation. Mum looked to be crying and shaking her head at what Bob was saying, at the sound of the door closing she looked up and beckoned me over. "My god I'm so sorry, I've killed us all, I'm so sorry" she kept repeating.

"Nonsense you weren't to know," said Dad trying to calm her down.

I nodded to them both indicating I knew.

Bob rose from the table leaving us to it as a family. As one we turned and went upstairs to our room.

"This can't be real, it's too real." Mum started to say.

"The car proved it Jen, it was no more real than a statue, the wheels were fixed and the doors didn't open. It was no more a car than the bench out there. We're here and we have to face it." He paused and looked at me, "How did you find out Pete?"

"It was Bex." The lie sprang straight out with no afterthought. "She had to let me know."

"My god what happened to her?" asked Mum.

"No one knows, her body is alive but no one can wake her, she's between worlds." I answered.

"Oh my, that poor dear, she's here alone?"

"No the vicar at the church looks after her."

"Poor dear." Her understatement reflected our own situation.

"So what happens now?" I asked anxious for a second opinion.

"Bob seems to think that we have been in a car accident and until we go one way or the other we could be stuck here. " said Dad. "They have a community here of people that are stuck and people who want to help. While we're here he asked if we would like to help out?"

Mum nodded her head and sighed, "That's what we plan to do until we know. One way or the other." She said rolling her eyes skyward.

We all climbed into bed that night in silence all faced with a different set of thoughts.

What was this power that Mehari spoke of? How could I use it, and what were these different realms he spoke of?

Fitfully I fell asleep dreaming of faceless creatures writhing in the dark of the cave.


**The Next Day**.


The next morning we awoke to the glow of sunlight peeking through the curtains. Dad rolled over and stuck his legs out of the bed. Mum stirred and turned over. By the huffing and puffing I could tell no one had slept well.

Dressed and ready we went downstairs into the bar. Bob and Trudy were waiting with breakfast ready on the table. We sat down and they joined us. Bob had a large steamy mug of coffee and a bacon sandwich. Trudy had tea and toast.

"Well today we'll have to see where we can put you two folks to help out. Is there anything you think you'd be good at, or would like to give a go?"

Dad shrugged and chewed a sausage. "Back in, well, the real world I work in an office, managing sales so that's going to be of little use, but Jenny here works in a bakery if that helps."

Bob smiled and raised a hairy eyebrow "As it happens there is a small bakery in town and I'm sure old Jeff that runs it could use a little help. For you Chris, maybe you could help out here. I can show you how to pour a pint, the rest is child's play."

Dad looked at Mum and then back at Bob. He nodded and said "OK then. I've been in enough pubs I'm sure that counts for something."

Bob laughed "Well you're keen, that's something I suppose. Trudy, after breakfast would you walk Jenny up to see Jeff at the bakery?"

"Of course I will lovey." she replied.

Bob looked at me, "I suppose we will have to leave you to roam the streets with the young lady from the vicarage, at least you know your old Dad will be here if you need him!" he laughed as I blushed a little at the mention of Bex.


After breakfast I slipped on my trainers and walked onto the street blinking in the sunlight. Behind me I could see Dad filling glasses with foam as Bob tried to teach him how to fill them with beer instead.

"Alright Pete, how did it go with the folks last night?" Bex had crept up behind me making me jump a little.

"As well you could expect I suppose. How did you take it when you found out?" I asked a little intrigued.

"I screamed until my throat was sore. Then I cried. I felt so alone, I didn't know when I would see Mum and Dad again, or my friends. I didn't know anyone here. I was so afraid of what would happen to me. But the vicar Benjamin was very patient. He's been here for many years now. He considers it his work for God to greet people as they arrive. He talks to them about this place and the others that they can go onto. I'm not sure if he's right but he was a great comfort to me when I first arrived." She looked at me as we walked down towards the river. "So what do you think Mehari  wants to teach you?"

"I have no idea, I'm not sure what this power is or how I'm supposed to use it. I'm only a boy, shouldn't  grown-ups be sorting this out?" I asked. I was a little afraid of what was going to happen, and of the unknown.

We reached the river and walked along it towards the willow tree and the cave behind where my destiny awaited.

Inside the cave it was gloomy. I leaned two hands against the wall and it lit up, it's golden glow illuminating the interior of the cave. Mehari sat cross legged on the floor his eyes shut. He looked asleep. Slowly his eyes opened and focused on me.

"Ah the Traveller returns. Good to see you again Traveller."

"Uh hi," I said "you can call me Pete."

"Very well Pete, and you Guide what you have me call you?"

"I'm Bex." she mumbled as she gazed about at the glowing rocks.

Mehari looked concerned. "Your name is too similar to an old foe of mine. I

do not like it. Have you another name Guide?"

"Um you could call me Rebecca, that's what Bex is short for."

Mehari nodded slowly, "That is much better. Pete and Rebecca the

Guide."

The glow from the walls was fading so I turned and placed my hands

against the wall, this time I waited until the glow had spread across every

surface. Mehari nodded again. "Very impressive Pete but we must train you to

harness your power. The power is not within you, it lives in the earth itself. In

order to harness it you will need to learn the ancient positions. These will

allow you to channel the power from the earth and shape it to your will. A

proper study of this could take years to master but I am afraid that we do not

have that long. The darkness grows."

Bex caught my eye and I stifled a giggle.

"Let us start with the basic stance. Please remove your shoes."

I knelt down and picked at the laces on my trainers. Kicking them to one

side I stood up straight. Mehari had adopted a pose like a boxer, feet flat on the floor one slightly ahead of the other. "Copy me please. Keep your feet flat to the floor, close your eyes and clear your mind. Feel the ground beneath your feet, imagine energy flowing up through your feet and filling your legs. Now concentrate on your stomach, feel power collecting there, filling you up to your chest. Slow your breathing and concentrate. Imagine, if you will, a powerful light radiating from the centre of your being. When you feel full of this power point your fingers and arms at the wall and will the power out of your body through your arms. Watch me for the movement."

Mehari moved with slow grace as he went through his motion. His eyes closed and his arms slowly raised to his chest, his hips turned and he pointed his arms at the wall. A crackle passed by us like someone dragged a nylon sheet over us. The fading light in the cave flared briefly before dimming again. I turned to press my hands to the wall.

"Wait, try the movement and motion I have just showed you to turn the light in here back on." Whispered Mehari. "Adopt the pose and relax into it. Feel the energy build within you then channel it at the cave."

I spread my feet like Mehari did. I slowed my breathing and shut my eyes. I could feel the hairs on the back of my neck standing on end. I suddenly felt full of power and whipped my arms up in shock. A loud crack and a blinding light followed. Trying to see through the glare it was apparent that the cave was lit as if by floodlight. Squinting I could see Mehari and Bex were slumped against the far wall, mere dark smudges in the blinding light. Despite being flung against a hard stone wall Mehari was laughing. "You truly are the Traveller Pete, you really are. Such power, now all you need is to learn some control."

"It was such a strange feeling within me, it came as a shock and I lashed out." I was buzzing from the experience. Never before had I had such a feeling.

"You must practice to get used to the feeling, you need to control the power. Don't let the feeling you get from the power overwhelm you. It is a seductive feeling but it must be controlled. If you let it take you then you open yourself to corruption." Mehari raised himself back to his feet.

"It was just so quick, I took the pose and it felt like I was full straight away." I gasped.

"Hmm maybe we need to use a buffer for training. Try putting your trainers back on."

I walked over to where my trainers sat next to Bex.

"That was unbelievable Pete, I flew across this cave when you whipped your arms forward. We were stood off to one side but everything around you

just flew where you pointed. And the light.... It was like staring at the sun."
She whispered breathlessly to me.

I pulled on my trainers and stood back up. I took my place next to
Mehari and together we adopted the pose. Feet apart one ahead of the other. I
shut my eyes and cleared my mind. This time instead of being full I could feel
myself filling like a glass under a tap. I raised my arms, turned my hips and
pointed at the wall. This time instead of a loud crack there was a fizz under
my skin running down my fingers. I could feel the power leave me. The light
grew bright around us and I kept my eyes tight shut until it had faded a little.

"Very good Traveller, control your breathing, allow your mind to stay
clear. Focus on the power moving through you." Mehari's words sounded like
they were coming from the other end of a tunnel. The ground before me
bulged and groaned then faded to black.

I opened my eyes again to find I was lying on my back. Bex was cradling
my head. "Whoa there Petey, you gave us all a bit of a fright there."

"Wha'.... what happened?" I stuttered.

"It often happens to new students. Channelling this type of power can
be very draining. The first time especially so." Mehari said. "Rest a while, that
is probably enough for today. Eat well tonight and we will resume practice

tomorrow. There is something I need to follow up, I believe I have had an insight thanks to your guide Rebecca here."

Bex looked chuffed. "You should have seen you Pete, wherever you pointed the air rippled like heat haze, and the walls glowed like you were pointing a hose of light at them. It was so cool."

I sat up and looked at Mehari, "Is there anything I can be doing tonight to practice?"

"Just clear your mind and be calm before you sleep. If you feel the power build in you try and let it go carefully. In this cave you are safe but out there is a different matter. The storm line is moving forward."

Mehari spoke these last words before turning towards the back of the cave. "Until tomorrow Pete." He then moved his body sideways and disappeared like he had walked through a doorway.

"Wow" we both said. Bex helped me to my feet and together we left the cave.

Outside the day was running out. "How long were we in there?" I asked.

"Time moves differently in the cave." Said Bex. I looked at her a little shocked. "Mehari explained it to me" she replied to my look.

Quietly we walked together back towards the town. The buzz of the power was winding down, I suddenly felt very hungry and wondered what was for tea.

"What are you having for your tea tonight?" I asked Bex.

"Don't know, the vicar might be a great man but he's not much of a cook." She made a face. "I think he boils everything, except on Sundays when one of the ladies in town delivers a roast meal to us."

"Do you want to join us at the pub for tea? It's Dads first shift there."

"That would be nice Pete but I have to get back before dark. Benjamin would only worry." Bex sounded a little disappointed.

We parted company at the front door of the pub, Bex running off calling back over her shoulder in a bad impression of Mehari "Until tomorrow Traveller!"

I opened the door of the pub and went inside.

Dad was behind the bar looking weary. His shift would be coming to an end soon. He put the glass he was drying up on the shelf above the bar and waved over at me.

"Hi Petey, have you and your friend been having fun?" I nodded yes and climbed onto a stool at the bar. "What's yer poison pardner?" he drawled in a pretty good cowboy voice.

"Two fingers of yer finest rot-gut." I drawled back.

He smiled and poured me out a coke. "That'll have to do you for now."

The door opened and Mum came through looking worn out from her day. "Hi Pete, I guessed you be here I've just seen Bex running up the hill to the church." She smiled at Dad.     "What's for tea today? I'm starving."
Dad handed over a couple of menus from behind the bar. "Whatever you and little britches here fancy purdy lady."

"Oh my, a pass from a handsome stranger." she said fanning her face.

We scanned the menu and ordered our tea.

A short while after Bob brought our food out,  he went and stood behind the bar, Dad came and joined us and we sat and ate our tea still talking like cowboys.


**Back in the Cave.**


The next day I awoke to the sunshine through the curtains. I rubbed my eyes to see Mum and Dad quietly getting dressed. We descended the stairs in a line and ate a small breakfast of  bacon and eggs. After clearing the table Dad started clearing up behind the bar, polishing the brass and setting out the bar towels. Mum wiped her face with a napkin then went and kissed Dad on the cheek. "I'll see you tonight Hun." She said turning and patting me on the head. "You walking me up the hill Pete?" I nodded I would. We both waved at Dad who waved back.

Outside the day was already growing warm. We walked slowly up the hill towards the bakery. At the door Mum waved me off and I walked on up towards the church lost in my own thoughts.   During the walk I reviewed my training with Mehari.  Every night I had tried to clear my mind of thoughts and be still but both nights I had found myself asleep and dreaming. Maybe today we could try it in the cave, see if that helped. Lost in thought as I was I didn't see Bex on the top step of the church waiting for me. As I got closer she jumped out on me shouting "BANZAI"

So lost in thought was I that I must  have jumped a clear foot off the ground. Stumbling backwards I struggled to stay on my feet.

"Got-cha napping" she grinned. Her eyes twinkled and her smile was so wide I imagined it would touch her ears.

"You did a bit, I nearly had a heart attack you made me jump so bad."

She skipped off down the hill her loose hair bouncing across her shoulders. I ran a little and caught her up.

"What do you reckon we'll be doing with Mehari today?" she asked.

"Dunno, but I need to try the clearing my mind thing, every time I try at home I fall asleep."

She laughed,"is your empty mind that dull Petey?" she laughed.

"Har dee har har, have you tried it? I lie in bed at night and clear my mind, or try to. The next thing I know I'm dreaming."

"The Vic had me cleaning the steps of the church last night when I got in so I was pretty bushed when I got to bed. C'mon I'll race you down the beach." She ran off down the beach towards the willow tree, legs kicking back as she ran.

I shrugged and followed suit. I ran harder than I had for a long while, but the beach was hard to run on, the loose surface made the footing uncertain. Soon my lungs burned on every breath but I was catching her up. Just before I caught her she slipped on a damp stone and fell to one knee. She gasped in shock as she fell. I reached her and skidded to a stop. Red blood bloomed from a scrape on one knee. I helped her up as she pressed her hanky to the small wound. She put her arm around my neck and together we hobbled over to the willow tree. Carefully we passed behind the trunk and into the gap leading to the cave.

In the middle of the cave sat Mehari the sound of his chant surrounding him, the walls glowing their pale yellow light. He looked up as we entered.

The hum stopped and the light faded so I pressed a hand to the wall, bathing the cave in a warm golden glow.

"Ah, you have both arrived. What is wrong Rebecca, are you hurt?" concern washed over his face as he rose taking her hand.

"I slipped running down the beach, it's OK."

"Let me see." he instructed.

She peeled away her hanky and a small trickle of blood ran down her leg.

"Sit," he gestured. As she did he rubbed his hands together, frowning in concentration he held his hands over the small wound and started his hum again. The tips of fingers glowed as his frown deepened. Bex gasped as he coughed and sat back. She licked her hanky and wiped away the blood that had gathered on her knee. Underneath the skin was unbroken.

"Wow, how did you do that? The pain is gone and I'm not bleeding."

"By manipulating the fabric of this place, using the power that flows through the Traveller and this place. What you see around you can be bent and controlled. The power or qi as it is properly known allows us to rebuild our reality in different ways. This control over the qi is what you must learn Peter." He coughed again. "It is a great exertion for me but for you with training it should be a breeze. In this place qi can easily be moulded to suit your purpose."

"In the cave?" I asked.

"No here in Styxworth. As a place between worlds the rules of your physical world don't apply as much. Now shall we begin today's training?"

I nodded and sat on the floor next to where Bex was still wiping her leg in amazement.

"To begin we shall meditate for a while, clear your mind traveller, relax your body. Do not let thoughts intrude as you relax and let go."

I cleared my mind and relaxed. I closed my eyes and tried not to think thoughts. After a short while I noticed that it seemed to be very bright around me. I opened my eyes and shut them almost instantly, the walls of the cave were alight, the golden glow was so bright it looked white. In that white space I had glimpsed two black shapes that of Mehari kneeling and composed and Bex with her arm shielding her eyes from the intense light.

The light started to fade a little to the point where I could open my eyes. Mehari opened his and nodded at me approvingly. "Good, the qi flows strongly through you. Now we shall try the positions of power once more. For this we shall adopt the position, hold it, but concentrate on keeping the light glowing in here, nothing more."

He rose to his feet and adopted the first position, feet spread like a boxer, arms by his waist. I copied him and together we went through the routine. Slowly, like a dance we moved from position to position. Throughout I could feel the power, or qi, bubbling up in me. Concentrating hard on the walls I left it bubbling away just enough, flowing out to keep the light in the cave walls glowing. We came to the end of the routine and the light dimmed a little.

"You are doing well young Traveller, you are learning control. When I feel you have mastered this we can move on to manipulating the world around us, shaping the qi to serve your purpose.

Practice this routine and the control over the coming days and when I return I will review your    progress."

"Return? Where are you going?" I asked.

"I have to leave Styxworth for a few days to determine where this threat to our balance is coming from. Hopefully it shall be a simple matter and easy to resolve. But in the meantime learn the positions and practice control." with these prophetic words he turned and melted into the spreading gloom of the cave.

"Wow!" said Bex, "What do you think all that meant?"

"I don't know but I think that we should get home. We can come back here tomorrow to practice."

We slipped out of the cave and behind the trunk of the willow tree. The sun hung low in the sky indicating it was late in the afternoon. "Race you back?" I asked smiling.

"Do you know, I think I'll walk this time."

We walked down the beach shoulder to shoulder. Climbing up the hill towards the Ferryman I felt tired and knew that I would sleep soundly again tonight.

I awoke the next day to a pale grey light coming through the curtains. Sticking my head through the gap I saw it was an overcast day. Mum and Dad were stirring and I quickly got dressed. After a breakfast of bacon sandwiches me and Mum left Dad setting up the bar of the Ferryman. We pulled the door to and stepped onto the quiet street. Looking down the street to the river I noticed people stopping and looking at the sky before swiftly moving on. In the distance a thick band of dark grey cloud could be seen. At a quick glance it looked like a distant mountain range that stretched across the horizon. "Looks like it's going to rain later Pete. Mind you don't get caught in it."

"Don't worry Mum I won't." I said thinking of the cool interior of the cave.

She ruffled my hair and walked off towards the bakers. I turned and headed up to the church.

At the steps of the church I met Bex with the vicar. Both looked concerned and were staring at the sky over the far bank of the slow moving river.

"Hey Pete, have you seen the clouds?" She asked.

"Yup, looks like it's gonna rain in a bit." I replied.

"I keep forgetting you've not been here that long." She said looking at me quizzically. "We don't tend to get rain or cloud or any other kind of weather here, that's why everyone is so concerned."

"And it's boiling up from across the river which is a cause for concern," said the vicar. "Maybe this is why the ferryman isn't sailing. He must have sensed this coming."

"What could it mean?" I whispered thinking of Mehari and his talk of balance and order yesterday.

"You two better play inside today, there are some games in the church hall, but keep the noise down I have some reading to do." The vicar said as he turned and headed back into the church.

"C'mon it's round the back here," she jumped off the step, grabbed my hand and ran off round the corner of the church. Behind the main building was a small hall that had clearly seen better days. The rough yellow walls were covered in a thick mat of ivy that was slowly being ripped down from its lofty position by the thorny tentacles of great bank of brambles. Small dirty windows were slowly being closed off by nature's assault and the corrugated roof was layered with a thick carpet of deep green moss.

Bex led me round to the door at the end of the building. Its peeling red paint flaked off as she pushed it open.

"The Vic doesn't keep it locked, there's no real point around here."

We stepped through the door into the gloom inside. The smell of mildewed and stale air hung in the air like damp sheets. With a flick of a switch Bex turned the lights on. They didn't do much to brighten the room. Rickety tables sat in groups with orange plastic chairs pushed under them. A door at the back of the hall led to a small kitchen, the serving hatch gaped open. Dust lay on every flat surface. To one side there was a wooden square on the floor that may have served as a dance floor at some distant point in the past. Bex started to move the tables off it with a loud scrape. I moved to help lifting the other side to stop the scraping. Quickly we piled the tables to one side and neatly stacked the chairs next to them.

"This place hasn't been used in a while."

"Nah I don't even think the Vic comes back here these days. I found it was open one day not long after I, well you know..."she paused, " I came in once but didn't like it so never came back. But I thought yesterday that it could be an ideal place to train." She skipped over to the kitchen and came back with a small stereo. "And I thought instead of just working through the 24 positions in grim silence like Mehari we could learn it like a dance with some music." She grinned and plugged it into a socket on the wall.

"Right first let's do the meditation and then we can see what the music is like." I said as I knelt down in the dust on the dance floor.
I cleared my mind and started to relax my body. A small surprised yelp from Bex made me open my eyes. She stood there in front of me covered in dust, grey from head to foot except her eyes shining out and her pink lips. She coughed and shook her head causing a cloud of dust to rise from her.

"Thanks Pete." She laughed shaking more dust from her hair.

"What happened?" I asked

"When you started to meditate all the dust around you rose up and moved away like a wave. I was in the way."

"Wow, ok I'll try again see I can knock it off you." I closed my eyes and let the thoughts fall from my mind. As a deep calm crept over my mind I let my muscles relax. I concentrated on my breathing slowing it down as Mehari

had shown me.

When I felt ready I opened my eyes and looked at the hall. It seemed brighter

and more welcoming than before. The deep layers of dust had gone and the

light filled the room rather than intruding on it.

"Right I'm ready to try the positions."

Bex nodded and hit the on button. Music filled the hall, loud cheery

music at a good tempo to move to. I adopted the starting position and Bex

followed suit. We moved together through the routine. My body automatically

taking to the routine leaving me to concentrating on controlling the qi

bubbling up inside me. At the end of the routine I held the final position, my

body trembling with the effort of containing the power inside me. My fists

glowed as I tried to stuff it all down inside. I shut my eyes and concentrated,

clearing my mind. For the second time a startled "oh" from Bex caused me to

lose focus. I opened my eyes to see that all the furniture in the room was

floating. I moved my hands this way and that watching as the tables and

chairs moved in time with my commands. I lowered my hands and the

furniture settled back on the floor.

I coughed and slumped to the floor exhausted.

"Wow that was quite something...." I gasped.

"Do you want to go again?" She asked.

"Not quite yet, I'm a little exhausted after that. Let's just sit a while."

Bex came and sat next to me on the floor. Some of the white dust from the room had stuck to her trainers. She looked around the room at the furniture that had been moved about and newly uncovered surfaces that had been covered in dust.

"So tell me about you Bex, how did you come to be here?"

"As Mehari said, there's not a lot to tell about me being here. My physical body is in a coma and I'm here while the doctors try to wake me up."

"Don't you miss being with your Mum and Dad?" I asked.

"I really do," her voice trembled with emotion, "but I try not to think of it. Sometimes at night when I'm asleep I see myself in the hospital and I can see my parents and friends around my bed. It's weird because I'm not looking through my eyes, it's as if I'm standing next to my body. I reach out and try to take my Mums hand and tell her that I'm ok but my hand passes straight through hers. Last time I thought she felt something because she looked at me, where I was, but she kept looking, searching for something she couldn't see."

We sat quietly for a bit, Bex struggling not to cry. Soon she jumped up, turned on the stereo and said a little to loudly, "come on then Pete, let's go through the routine again, but this time I need to see you move properly. You dance like a puppet with tangled strings." She giggled as she mimed a marionette dancing.

I laughed and rocked onto my feet. Brushing some dust from the rubber shell toe of my trainer I stood straight and rolled my shoulders and cracked my knuckles.

"Right, feel the beat of the music Pete. Step in time."

I stepped in what I thought was time to the music. Bex doubled up in laughter pointing at me. "You look like your wading through deep water. Stop plodding about, and let the music move you."

"I'm trying but I don't like dancing, it's girls stuff."

"Nonsense, all girls like a guy who can dance. Now stop. No stop plodding Pete you're killing me......" Again she dissolved into fits of giggles. She straightened and tucked a loose curl of hair behind her ear.

"Let's start with the beat, tap it out with your foot. Listen to it, pick up the tempo, that's it" she smiled as my foot stopped twitching randomly and picked up the beat. "Now alternate the beats with your feet, shuffle them back and forward."

Once more she bent over in laughter. "What now, I've picked up the beat? I think I'm getting this." I said.

"Pete, it looks like your arms have been nailed on, move them come on that's it like me Pete." She started to move about shaking her arms and legs in time with the music.

"I'm not sure my limbs can do that!" I said in awe as she skipped past me. She grabbed my hands and started moving me back and forwards, shaking my arms and shifting my feet.

"That's it you just need to loosen up a bit. Get that pole out of your butt. See we're dancing."

I closed my eyes a little a let the music wash over me. Moving along to the music felt good and it felt right. A now familiar sensation bubbled up through me.

"Er Pete, let's just take it down a notch, Eh?"

I opened my eyes to see that we were dancing together, but a foot off the ground. I coughed and shrugged and we dropped to the ground.

"Your moves are getting there but you need to work on your landing." Bex laughed. Right then Mr, are you ready to try the positions again, but this time with some extra funk?"

I nodded. I closed my eyes and cleared my mind, the next song started and Bex turned the volume up a bit. I started by tapping out the rhythm with my feet, then once I had the beat I made fists and jumped into the first position, feet apart like a boxer I started the routine. But this time something

was different, the moves flowed from one to the other, the power inside didn't

bubble and jerk it seemed to flow in and around me, my fists glowed and my

hair stood on end. At the end of the routine I held the final position, stood on

one foot, the other hanging in the air in front of me arms aloft. I closed my

eyes and held it as the qi lapped around me like water at the edge of a lake,

gentle enough but with an untapped mass behind it.

Presently I opened my eyes and looked round at Bex. She smiled and

clapped. "Wow, that final position you were hovering two feet off the ground.

And you were glowing..... Wow."

The air felt charged as if someone had pulled a nylon jumper over us.

Bex turned the stereo down and we sat down on the floor again.

"I'm hungry, shall we go down to the bakery and see if we can get a cake

from Mum?"

Bex nodded. We stood and walked out of the hall. The sky outside was

dark and foreboding.   A clear line of cloud cut across the sky giving the light

a funny hue. Everything seemed more yellow, a sickly jaundiced yellow. It

made me think of the time last summer when we had gone to visit my elderly

aunt in hospital. She had been propped up in bed to receive visitors. She was

losing the battle to a liver disease. She had been a large woman in life, domineering and bossy. Now she had been reduced in size and stature, her whole essence had been diminished. No longer was she the woman who's shout induced terror but an old and frail woman. We stood next to her bed Mum and Dad talking about everyday things as if we were meeting for a cup of tea. I wanted to shout that she was ill could no one see. But I couldn't. I was transfixed by her decline in appearance, her skin, which had always been fine and rosy, hung off her face like cheap wax clinging to the skull underneath. Her hair was going see through and you could see the scalp beneath. The various tubes and probes linking her to machines gave me the impression that she was becoming more machine than human, that the hospital machine taking away her blood for cleaning was somehow taking away her spirit as well. I shivered at the memory.

Bex stopped and looked at the sky and whispered two words to herself "Storm line."

I looked at her but she shook her head as if trying to clear it and skipped down the steps at the front of the church.

We ran down the hill to the bakery where Mum was working. As we ran down the hill we ran about and around each other, hiding in doors and dodging up alleyways. After a few minutes we skidded to a halt outside the bakery door. Mum was behind the counter putting a loaf into a paper bag for a lady. She turned, saw us through the glass and gave a cheery wave. The lady put her loaf into a shopping bag and left. We piled in through the door.

"Good afternoon, Lady, Gentleman. How may I be of service to you this fine day?" Said Mum putting on a very grand voice.

"Have you got any cakes you could let us have?" I asked.

"Pete it's two hours 'til dinner, can you not wait?"

"But Mum we're starving. I'm not sure I'll make it through 'til dinner...." I implored smiling at her.

"Oh I didn't realise it was critical! Now that you say it you both appear to be fading before my eyes." She rummaged for a paper bag and put two custard tarts in. "I'm sure Jeff won't mind. Bex would you like to come to dinner with us tonight?"

"That's very kind but the Vic will want me back before dark. Especially if there's a storm coming." We all turned to look out of the window at the storm line.


**Mehari's return**.


The next day morning crept into the room barely lighting the corners. We dressed in near silence and trooped downstairs for breakfast. After we ate me and Mum headed out the door and up the hill. Halfway up I heard a shout

and saw Bex barreling down the hill towards me.

"Come on Pete, we're heading this way today." She yelled as she flew

past me.

Mum gave me a quick peck on the cheek and I turned a gave chase. As

we got to the wall along the river bank I caught her up. We stopped, breathing

heavily and catching our wind.

"I love running down that hill, I think if I run quick enough nothing can

catch me, and one day maybe I'll break through or wake up....." Said Bex

between deep breaths.

I grinned at her not really knowing what to say. Maybe she could break

through or wake up. I changed the subject instead. "Any reason we're playing

down here today?" I asked.

"I think I had a message from Mehari last night, I think he's back from

his travels."

"What kind of message?" I asked a little put out that he hadn't contacted

me.

"This." She said reaching into her pocket. She pulled out an ancient

looking coin. Turning it over and over in her hand I could see a picture of an

old man and some oriental looking writing.

"It was on my pillow when I went to bed last night. The window was closed and the Vic said no one had been around during the day. It's odd but I know it's from him."

I agreed and we climbed over the wall and dropped onto the beach. We walked quickly along the beach keeping away from the water which looked ominous and dark without the sun shining on it. We arrived at the tree and Bex slipped round the trunk and into the cave first. I followed after. As I entered the cave I ran my hands along the walls giving light to the dim interior. As expected Mehari was there in the middle of the cave.

He sat cross legged on the floor with the soles of his feet pointing to the ceiling. His hands rested in his lap like the statues of the Buddha I had seen on a museum visit once. His beard was tatty and his hair unkempt. His robe seemed dusty like he had been sleeping rough. As we entered and lit the cave his eyes opened and he regarded us.

"Ah good you got my message Rebecca." His voice was as dry and dusty as his robes. "Come and sit with me. I have travelled far and wide and I believe I know what is coming. I also think I  know who is behind this. We have our work cut out Traveller." He regarded me with his knowing eyes as we sat in front of him. He began to speak.

"This place that you find yourselves in is not just a creation of man. This limbo is a place inhabited by men such as you but also to the ancient races that went before. Across the river is the land of the dead where all go to rest, but this place, this limbo is a holding area for those nearly and newly departed. The shock of death can be damaging to anyone who experiences it. Some are ready to leave but most need a little time to come to terms with it. That is why Styxworth is here. It serves as a buffer to calm the troubled mind of those who arrive. When they are ready they will pay Charon the ferryman and he will take them to the land across the water ready for the next life."

He stood up at this point and stretched his legs out. He ran a hand through his hair and tugged at his long beard. "Pete do you remember when you arrived, the townsfolk broke the news to your parents that although their bodies were in a critical condition their non physical form was ok? That is what Styxworth's purpose is. Rebecca I'm sure you remember the same.

Since the more ancient races lived many years before mankind they have nearly all moved on, to the land across the river. Some of these people though can move back and forward across the divide. People such as myself, we try to maintain balance in this realm. Violent types are removed to their own place and those of a more pleasant nature are sent to theirs. Your world knows a little of this. Religions talk of heaven and hell, but these are simplistic terms. The arrangements are much more complicated and serve to establish balance and harmony. But there are those who seek to tip the balance in their favour, for fun, or for malevolent purpose it matters not. In times of unbalance two sides emerge. On the malevolent side are those that seek chaos, imbalance, and anarchy. But on the other side are those who seek calm, balance, and harmony. This is always the way, and is part of the nature of balance itself. In order to to appreciate the light there must be dark and if my suspicions are correct, it may be dark for some time.

On the side of chaos this time is an unruly sort, a truly ancient being, a demon called Jex. He is the reason I cannot call you Bex young Rebecca. He is a vain, arrogant being that thrives on times of chaos. He is not normally at the forefront of the action as his stupidity matches his arrogance. I have this feeling that someone or something else is behind this latest attempt to tip the scales." He sat down on the floor, the glow started to fade so I rubbed a hand on the wall.

In the fresh light I could see the concern etched onto Mehari's face. "This time it feels different. Before he has been a trickster, small annoyances that were easily sorted out, but this time....." His words faded away.

"What can we do?" I asked. "Is that why I'm here?"

"In the past it has mostly been small matters, a possession here, a haunting there, but this..... It feels too big for Jex alone, but he is the one we must face. As a united front we should be able to overturn this storm of chaos and restore the balance to this realm." He sighed and rubbed a hand over his face. He looked tired and worn out. "We should rest first, a small dose of meditation should help, especially here in this cave. Whenever one of us on the side of order is in need of recuperation we come here. It restores us, helps us to endure. It has never been breached to this day by the agents of chaos. Come Traveller sit a while, you too guide. Let us meditate and hope for answers."

We sat in the fading light of the cave, silent, thoughts focused on the future and what it may bring to us.

Mehari let out a long sigh that brought us round from our silent thoughts. "Come let us return to our lodgings for the night. I will accompany you up to the village edge."

We rose as one together and exited the cave. The light was beginning to grow dim and had a strange hue to it, no doubt from the storm clouds coming in from the other side of the river. We walked down the beach in silence, but at the steps up to the street Mehari stopped and turned to us both.

"Tonight I want you both to meditate before sleep and see if any visions or thoughts come to you. Especially you Guide, we need you to lead the Traveller on the right path." He looked closely at us both before turning back towards the cave. "Until tomorrow then."

We raised a hand in farewell and turned up to the village. We walked slowly up the street towards the Ferryman quietly, both of us lost in thought.

"What do you suppose Mehari meant by visions?" I asked.

"I'm not sure," said Bex sounding uneasy, "But something was coming to me in the cave, but it was keeping out of reach, like when you can't think of the right word to say."

I looked at her "Go on...."

"I don't know yet but I think I'm close to it, hopefully it'll come to me in the night." She shook her head and turned to smile at me, "Well see you tomorrow Petey!"

She skipped up the street with a wave over her shoulder and I put my hand on the door of the pub and pushed it open.

**The Corruption**

The next day dawned, the light through the window was grey and gloomy. We all dressed quietly and Dad led us downstairs to breakfast. After a light breakfast of cereal me and Mum left through the front door. To my surprise Bex was sitting on the step waiting for me. "You two run along and play safe okay?" Mum shouted after us as we ran off towards the river.

"I think I know a little more about what's happening." Said Bex as we reached the sandy beach. The sun was trying to press through the clouds but the weak light cast no shadows. We walked along the river towards the cave. "I dreamt about a man I don't know last night. He was a bad man dressed in white. His words were false and his face didn't seem to fit." We reached the tree before the cave.

"Let's talk to Mehari, he might know more about it." I said as I squeezed into the cave. I pressed a hand against the wall and was not surprised to see Mehari sat in the middle of the cave. The sudden light from the walls caused Mehari to open his eyes and greet us both.

"Well Guide did anything come to you in the night?" Mehari asked his eyes alive with interest.

"I think so, I was just telling Petey about a dream I had last night. I dreamt of a bad man dressed all in white. His face didn't seem to fit, it was if it was alive in some way. He was talking to a crowd of people and they were believing him, cheering him on. I was trying to shout at them, tell them he was deceiving them but they couldn't hear me. It felt like I was trapped behind glass and I was starting to melt. My legs sank into a puddle in the concrete and I couldn't raise my arms. That's when I woke up." She had been staring straight ahead as she told us of her dream, almost as if she was reliving it. As she finished she shook her head freeing the hair she had tucked behind her ear. "It was horrible, the people couldn't see or hear his lies. No one could help me."

"That is how Jex works. He tells people pretty lies they want to hear, half truths to get his way, to gain control. He may come to each person in Styxworth and tell them things to embarrass and enslave them. Imagine if he came to you and told you that he would tell everyone your darkest secret. All you had to do to prevent this would be one small act to stop him. One harmless little favour and never would he speak your hearts darkest secrets. How many would crumble? The trouble is he doesn't know anything. Not really, but many people will be fooled by him and taken in by him. Chaos and darkness will cloud the streets of this place if he is not stopped quickly. Young Rebecca you may dream of the other being working with Jex tonight, if you do we will need to hear about it."

Bex nodded her face stern but her lip trembled, just a little but it was there.

"Today then we must see if we can learn to fight. Are you ready Traveller? Are you ready to harness the qi energy around you and banish the demon from these lands?"

I nodded to Mehari that I was. "Okay, we need to break down the positions you have been learning as a routine into their individual parts. The first two positions, adopt them for me now." I started to hum and struck the first position, feet shoulder width apart fists clenched arms by my side, then I moved it into the second position feet slightly in front of one another fists raised.

"These are the first two combat stances. While physical confrontation is not to be recommended, the physical form helps to harness the qi energy for combat. From here you can strike with either arm directing energy, and from position two you have a sturdier stance in case of frontal attack. I am going to throw some pillows at you now, make sure they don't hit you by using qi only." He gently threw the first pillow directly in front of me, an easy target. I concentrated and flung a fist at it. A rush of energy went through me and down my arm and the pillow disintegrated in a flash of blinding light. "A little keen, try not to destroy these pillows, control at all times must be your watchword." He threw the next one and I flung my arm out again working hard to reel in the power I could feel crackling around me. With a crack like a whip the pillow shot across the cave hitting the far wall where it left a glowing imprint. "Very good, Traveller, again. This time stance two."

I jumped into the position and shot the pillow across the cave. "Will it matter the size or weight of the target how much force I need to use?" I asked.

"In this realm nothing really has weight or mass, it is only your perception and memory of the physical world that define your experience here." I looked at him confused. "Something is only heavy here because you expect it to be, that is your minds memory of it. It is the same for all things here. Bacon tastes of bacon because you expect it to. Milk tastes of milk because that is how you remember it. Nothing is really real here, it is the way it is because that is the way you need it to be. The best Travellers are always younger because unlearning the way the physical world worked is easier than for adults. Children are surrounded daily by the magic and mystery of the technological age and their imagination hasn't yet been ruined by the world around them." Mehari gazed at me. I thought I understood.

"So my memories of things make them real here?" I asked.

"In a way. Styxworth acts as a buffer between the living and the worlds beyond, it meets your expectations. You expect a car to be heavy, so it is. If you can unlearn that memory or expectation then the car ceases to be heavy. But the difference between saying you know, and believing is a very great one."

"I think I get it, but for now let's blast some pillows." I struck the first combat stance and spent the morning sending pillows around the room. After I while I began to be able to aim them, sending them flying at Bex as she ran away from them giggling.

"I think you have practiced that enough for today, next come positions three and four. I ran through the routine in my head. Position three was similar to position two, feet in front of one another, but with my weight over the back foot. Hands raised at face level. Position four was feet spread at shoulder level arms crossed in front of my chest. Head dropped but eyes up.

"Good, never take your eyes off of your opponent. Not for a second, Jex is a master of lies and confusion, he will try anything to fool you should you meet him in combat. These two positions are defensive positions. You can use them to form a barrier of qi around yourself to protect from incoming attacks. Again we will practice with these cushions. Take stance three, and concentrate on trying to form a barrier, do not shoot your energy try to focus it into a shield." With that he threw the first cushion. I held my hands in the position and focused my thoughts into a shield. Keeping my eyes on the approaching

cushion I was able to watch it until it hit me in the face.

"What happened there, I was concentrating on forming a shield?" I

spluttered.

"This discipline is much more difficult than firing off bolts of energy, it

requires focus and concentration, relax your mind, adopt the stance and we

try again, Rebecca would you like to join me in testing the Traveller?" Mehari

asked, smiling a little.

"After being a target for flying cushions all day I am gonna enjoy this!"

She said grabbing a couple of Mehari's pillows.

For the next twenty minutes or so I stood in the middle of the cave

focusing on producing a shield to protect myself while being hit in the head

from all sides by many colourful pillows. Eventually after a great deal of

sweating on my behalf and even more laughing from Bex I managed to stop a

pillow before it hit me square between the eyes. "At last!" I shouted, losing

concentration and being hit by another shot from Mehari. I quickly readopted

the stance and my focus. Soon the pillows were bouncing off an invisible

shield around me.

"Stance four will produce much the same effect but can be useful for

moving through the next two positions. These are for counter attacking and are also for tomorrow. Come, we shall end today's session with a little meditation, Guide if any visions occur do not hesitate to tell us."

Gratefully we sat on the cool stone of the cave floor and in the dimming light from the walls we closed our eyes and relaxed our minds. Concentrating on slowing our breathing the way Mehari had showed us, focusing on a single image to clear our minds of everyday chatter. I began to feel the light and floaty way you feel just before sleep, until a scream from Bex brought us back to our senses. "There's a man with the bad man, he's laughing at us. I can't see his face, it looks like it's behind a veil, and there are creatures moving in the clouds." She sighed and opened her eyes, looking almost surprised to still be in the cave.

"This doesn't bode well." Muttered Mehari below his breath. "Come, I will walk you back along the beach." We rose and left the cave.

As we walked along the beach in the grey light of the early evening I looked at the river. It appeared to be rougher than normal. "Mehari, why is the river getting rougher, does it have anything to do with the creatures that live in it?"

"What do you know of those who dwell in the river Peter?" Asked Mehari.

"Nothing really, I just remember when me and Dad arrived we were skimming stones and I saw a hand grab one of my stones as it bounced on the water."

"In the river dwell the memory remains of those who cannot pass over. Those who became lost. They didn't live a good life and did not want to go back to try again, they wander around between realms neither living nor passing on. Eventually they will wash out the end of the river and become one with the eternal. But until then they reside in the river. I sense they are becoming agitated by something or someone. This again does not bode well. Guide, when you dream tonight try and remember as much of it as you can."

"I don't even know if I want to go to sleep, I got the feeling he, or it can see me in there." Bex shivered as she thought of her recent vision.

"I understand your concern but for now you must remain strong, we need you to see so we may follow." Mehari placed his hands on her shoulders and looked into her eyes. After a pause she met his gaze and nodded.

"I can do this. I don't want to but I can do this." She nodded again and Mehari followed suit.

We had reached the steps up to the street and we parted. Mehari turned and moved swiftly down the beach. Me and Bex slowly wandered up the street, kicking a small stone between us.

"Is this guy really as bad as you say?" I asked.

"I guess so, he just comes to me as a bad man, like the one your parents try to scare you with, you know how they'd say 'don't do that or the bad man will get you'? Well I think I've just seen the bad man." She shivered again and pulled the zip on her hoodie up. The rest of the short walk up the hill we were silent, lost in our own thoughts. At the door to the Ferryman Bex squeezed my hand , whispered "stay safe." And ran off up the hill towards the church.

## Training continues

"Concentrate Peter!" The booming voice of Mehari echoed around the cave as another cushion flopped at my feet. I shook the sweat from my eyes and ran my fingers through my hair. Today's training session was proving to be more arduous than yesterday's. We were working on counter attacking, turning defence into offence. I was struggling to convert my qi from a defensive to offensive form quickly enough to be effective. I could block the cushions using the defence stance and the counter attack stance but I couldn't turn it to attack. I ended up grabbing at the cushions or swatting them away with my arms. "Stop seeing the cushions with your eyes. Stop seeing them as physical objects. Use your mind and your qi instead, defend and attack at the spiritual level." Mehari's voice sounded exasperated. "Come sit and meditate a while."

We sat on the cold floor of the cave. Looking over at Bex pale face I got the feeling she wasn't sleeping well. I think images of the bad man had been plaguing her dreams. I crossed my legs and let my thoughts float away from me. Mehari's soothing voice guided us to a more relaxed state.

Some time later he stood up. "I have it. Do you remember when you told me about how you were training up at the church hall?" I nodded, "You and Rebecca were dancing and you found you were floating?" Again I nodded. "Maybe we can use this as an aid to shaping your qi. You were distracted and used your qi to raise you up in the air, but you did it at a sub-conscious level. When we meet here tomorrow can you bring your music machine, we shall see if this over comes the problems Peter seems to be having?" Bex nodded.

"Yeah sure, I'll bring it and we can make Pete dance for us." She said as she suppressed a fit of the giggles. I threw a cushion at her which she swatted away.

"Tell me Rebecca did you dream anymore of our adversary last night?" Asked Mehari.

"Yes, I still can't see his face but his clothes and his manner are distinct. He appears clothed as a man but I don't think he is. Something moves behind his skin, like he is trying to hide his real form, and I think you can almost see it if you look away. If you see him out of the corner of your eye you may see his real form. I don't mean to be this vague but that's how he appears. Other than that he speaks falsely and no one seems to know. His words are like his image false, shifting, appearing as that which you would want them to be. He tells you what you want to hear, that's how he tricks you." Bex shuddered as she spoke. Her voice was flat like she was reading, the memories obviously difficult for her. "It's like I've seen him before, not here but before when I was...." Here she stopped as a tear formed at the corner of her eye. "Mehari, could he be the reason I'm here? Did he hurt me in the real world?" She asked, her voice lifting as the images clicked in her head.

"I do not know but I fear that may be so. From what you've told me I believe this being to one known simply as The Corruption. A being of malevolent intent. He infests and controls other bodies to suit his purpose. He is truly ancient, from before even my race. When he and his kind were stalking the Earth there was no good or evil, there was simply life. Some helped preserve it and others took it away. As life moved on and we gained a moral sense creatures like The Corruption were locked away in the deepest reaches of the afterlife but they get out, they feed on human misery. We can only hope that he can be put back and kept there. The Corruption has not infested Jex but he whispers in his ear from another body. No wonder the

idiot demon is being so bold." Mehari grew quiet at this point and sat back

down.

I looked at Bex and she in turn looked back at me. We shrugged at each

other then turned back to look at Mehari. "We are here to help lock this

Corruption up in any way we can Mehari." I said.

"I hope that we can Traveller, I hope that we can. Now go, take the

afternoon off, but be aware of anything lurking in the shadows, Jex and his

kind do not like the direct sun but this cloud will bring out the devil in them."

We needed no further invitation and headed out of the cave and onto

the beach by the churning river. We walked towards the town not saying

much to each other, reflecting on what Mehari had said about The

Corruption. When we reached the Ferry we noticed a small crowd of people

milling around. They looked as if they were trying to form a queue but people

were taking turns to sit on the floor and a nearby bench. They looked grey,

everything from their clothes to their skin and their big sad eyes. We hopped

up to the path but they didn't seem to see us. The Ferry was not open and a

line of people was beginning to form.

"If the Ferryman doesn't sail soon, imagine what this is going to be

like." Said Bex. I remembered bits from TV news about refugee camps in

Africa. I shook at the thought. I was about to speak when one of the grey men stood up and walked to the edge of the river. He turned and surveyed the camp with his sad grey eyes then jumped into the tumultuous water. He tried to swim but the water appeared to boil around him as hands shot out from under the surface and pulled him under. His expression didn't change as he was pulled under. The only sound was a small scream from Bex. None of the other people queuing at the ferryman's terminal seemed to notice or care.

"Let's go up and see the Vic quickly" I said turning and grabbing Bex arm. She followed walking slowly the shock of seeing the man pulled under filled her limbs with lead.

At the door to the church we caught up with the Vic who was sweeping the step. He lay his brush against the iron railing of the church and gave us a jaunty wave as we walked up. One look at Bex stopped his wave halfway. "What happened to her?" He asked taking Bex by the arm and guiding her into the little house to one side of the church. We took her inside and sat her on the couch, a big saggy but surprisingly comfy chair covered in cushions. Bex curled up next to one of the large arms and grabbed a large cushion hugging it to herself. Her eyes were wide and staring. The Vic made some tea. He set the steaming mugs on the table and I told him about what had happened at the river.

"Who are those people, and why were they so keen to cross the river, and why could they not see us?" I had a stream of questions popping up through my brain like bubbles and I was trying to ask them all at once.

"The grey people are those who come here that are ready to move on. Unlike you or Bex who need some adjustment, these people don't. They are ready to cross the river to the afterlife. Normally Charon, the ferryman, would take them across but he is not sailing. The cloud and the river have stopped his boat crossing. If he doesn't start again soon I don't know what we will do. More souls may be lost to the ever flowing river." The Vic sighed and sipped at his tea.

"So if one of the grey people jump into the river they will be dragged under, and along, but to where?"

"Nothingness. Once a soul is lost to the river it washes out into a sea of nothing. Some souls are ready to go, those are the hands you saw, and some are damaged beyond a capacity to perceive an afterlife. These are washed away to the endless sea." He appraised me with his eyes to see if I had got his point.

"How can a soul become nothing?" I asked

"Drop a drip of your tea in the river and watch it become nothing. It becomes part of the sea and nothing more."

"It seems a cruel way to go." I said slightly appalled at the thought.

"It's worse than cruel, like much of the universe it is simply indifferent, and as you get older you will realise that that is worse than ever." The Vic inhaled and stood. "Do you need me to walk you back to the pub before it gets dark Pete?"

"No I want to think about what I've seen and what you've said."

"Thank you for being a friend to Bex, she has been lonely since she came here. Head straight home now Pete." He waved as I set off down the hill towards the Ferryman.

Lost deep in thought I nearly jumped out of my skin when a hand landed on my shoulder.

"Hey Petey, penny for your thoughts!" It was Mum who had just finished at the bakery and was walking to our home.

"I'm not sure I'm done thinking them yet." I said

"Ooooh sounds deep, what do you fancy for your tea tonight? I'm hoping there is some ham left over, I just fancy ham, egg and chips. And as a treat Jeff gave me some left over sticky buns!"

I smiled, took Mum's hand and walked down the cobbled street toward the pub.

## Dance Training

The morning light outside the pub was grey and weak. As I opened the door I found Bex sat waiting for me on the step. Her hair looked unkempt and her eyes were red. In her hand she held her portable stereo for the days training.

"Morning Pete." She sighed.

"Are you ok Bex?" I asked concerned at her appearance.

"Didn't sleep well, I was meditating before bed and I kept seeing the grey man in the river. I couldn't concentrate, all I could see was his face. His expression never changed Pete. It was like he didn't know, or worse care." Her voice hitched a little. "After a while I began to doze and I dreamt of The Corruption. It felt like it was looking for me. I kept dodging away from his gaze but I could here it laughing while while it searched."

"Wow, and I thought the bakers stale buns were bad!"

Bex looked at me, hurt showing in her eyes, but a smile beginning at the corners of her mouth. She saw my grin and we both began to laugh softly together.

"Sometimes Pete you can be such a prat. If your not careful I'll guide you off a cliff." She said laughing harder now.

I mimed walking with my eyes shut and my arms outstretched. "Yes master" I drawled in my best monster voice.

Bex stood and walked after me down towards the beach. As we neared the river we could see the ranks of grey people around the dock had swelled over night. Desperate faces gazed out over the river and a few looked like they were preparing to jump. The laughter that had started so easily up the hill died as we saw them.

"Do you think Mehari knows about these guys?" Bex asked.

"I have no idea but I think he needs to."

We hastened our step onto the beach and hurried towards the cave hiding behind the tree.

Inside the cave the walls glowed dimly. Mehari sat in his meditating position in the middle of the floor. A soft him resonated from him and the light from the walls rose and fell with its pitch. I gently laid a hand on the cold stone bringing the light up brighter and brighter. Mehari stopped humming and opened an eye. He smiled warmly at us both and stood in one fluid motion.

"Good morning to you both. I see Rebecca has come prepared to make music, perhaps this can inspire our Traveller to focus his qi today!" He smiled again as he perused us both.

"Before we start do you know what is happening down at the ferry. The Ferryman is not sailing and a queue is forming." I gushed, eager to inform Mehari of the latest turn of events.

"Hmm this is a worrying turn of events. Soon they will grow restless and begin to try and swim the river." He said thoughtfully stroking his beard. A small gasp from Bex caught his attention. "Ah, I see that that is already the case. Then we must speed our plans forward. Today's training may well be the last for now. I fear Jex will appear before the townsfolk before to long with his offer of answers."

"What could his answers be?" Bex asked.

"What any person in a position of power offers. Half truths and lies designed to strengthen their own position while hiding the real problem. He may calm the river or part the clouds, but only if a service is performed for him. People always want an easy answer and he will offer it."

"What can we do though?" I asked.

"Against his gilded words and strength of feeling not a great deal. We have to work at the source of the problem, we have to dislodge the hold The Corruption has over Styxworth and unseat the demon. Only by shining truth on his dark words can we hope to show people what he truly is. Hopefully this will be enough." Mehari hung his head as the weight of the challenge we would be facing dawned upon him.

"But all that is for later, Rebecca I see you brought your music machine. Let's see if we can train this Traveller up a little."

Bex set up her portable stereo and pressed play on the front. Music flooded the cave with the happy sound of pop. Mehari sighed a little and shook his head. "The things you kids listen to..." He sighed again and picked up some of the cushions from yesterday's training session.

After a couple of hours I could bounce the cushions off a shield of pure qi and aim them where I wanted. Defend and counter. Flinging a few at Mehari I soon grew bored as his mastery of his qi caused them to fall flat at his feet but Bex had no such training. She was soon leaping and ducking as I sent cushion after cushion flying at her. She squealed as one tangled her feet and she fell over. "The batteries are starting to run down. The music's getting quieter."she said as she stood and brushed herself off.

"Give them to me." Mehari held his hand out. Bex snapped the cover off the back of the stereo and handed Mehari the batteries. He rubbed them between his hands and blew into his cupped palms. Squeezing them hard he frowned in concentration. Around us the walls of the cave pulsed a little brighter. "There you go try them now." He said as he handed them back to Bex.

"Good as new." She said as the music came back older than ever making us jump a little.

"We had a worthwhile training session today Peter, we shall meditate before I bid you farewell for today. Rebecca sit and see if you have any insight about our foe."

Bex swallowed hard and sat down between us, closing her eyes and letting her shoulders sag a little. I too sat and closed my eyes. I concentrated on slowing my breathing and clearing my mind. The light in the cave dimmed as we relaxed although the level of light rose and fell with my breathing. Inhale, exhale, qi shifted and moved. I opened my eyes and blew at the wall nearest to me. A bright spot glowed on the stone wall before spreading slowly and becoming one with the light. I was reminded of Mehari's talk of souls washed down the river to the sea. A calmness spread through me. My mind became clear and my eyes heavy. All that was in my mind was smoke and light. Smoke turning slowly in a shaft of light. A memory of my great grandfather and his pipe. So real I could smell the tobacco he used. I wondered if he had crossed the river and where he was now. The thought brought comfort to me.

"He's coming. He's walking into the town, he's talking to people." I started as Bex spoke. Her voice was lower than normal as though she were asleep. "The false man in the white suit is walking through the town. He comes to the people promising resolution to the current problems of the town. They can't see his words are false. The Corruption drives him but is not with him. It has taken a human form. It comes soon. If we can destroy his human form he can be sent back to the pit. We will soon see his face." Bex slurred these last words and slumped forward in a faint. Mehari lay her down cradling her head in his hand. He murmured in his strange tongue, his face drawn in concentration. Bex eyes flickered and she sat up. She seemed a little surprised to be laid out on the floor. As she sat she old us what she had seen.

"I saw him, Jex, he's coming into town just like you said Mehari."

"We know Bex, you just told us." I said to her.

"I couldn't have, I've just finished the vision I had." She looked a little concern.

"Wherever you receive your visions from may have been speaking to us through you. Remember when I told you about The Corruption I said there were others that were the complete opposite? Well I think one of those may be guiding you Bex. Don't fight it let it talk through you. In your heart you will know the difference between the good and the bad beings out there. If it feels wrong then fight but if not then let the energy of the other flow through you.

You never know when it could be useful." Mehari sat back on his heels

stroking his beard a strange twinkle in his eye.

"Should we go to town and challenge Jex?" I asked eager to set about

our quest.

"No Traveller. If you were to appear in town, the child who had recently

arrived with his parents, confronting the man who promised to sort out the

problems, how do you think you would fare? People would turn on you while

Jex made you out to be the source of the problems. You would be banished,

the clouds would be parted and Jex would be in charge. We need to ignore the

weed and kill the root. We need to find The Corruption and force him back to

the pit. Guide did you see a face or a person when you were shown The

Corruption?"

"I saw him as a man, blue jeans and a t shirt, he has no hair, there was

something familiar about him. Like I've seen him before somewhere. I think

he is outside of town, raising the creatures of the pit to play in the clouds and

stirring the water in the river. I think he is at the other end of the beach near

the edge of the ocean." Her eyes snapped up from the floor to Mehari's face.

"That's where she showed him to me."

"She?" I asked.

"It's definitely a female voice that spoke to me or through me. She's old but she is of the light. I see her in saffron robes with rosy skin. Sorry it's all a bit vague but all I get is pictures and abstract images. But The Corruption is dressed as a man and at the other end of the beach. I'm sure of it."

**The Ocean.**

"We cannot afford to move against The Corruption tonight. His kind are stronger in the dark. Also I would like to see what Jex is up to in the town, how well his lies are being spread around."

We left the cave and Mehari followed wearing a dark Cape that I hadn't seen before. The swell around the pier had swelled considerably and in the evening sun another grey body was silhouetted standing on the rail above the water. He turned and as he fell gracefully backwards into the raging water Bex buried her face into Mehari's cloak. As she did a darkness fell across her body.

"What kind of a cloak is that Mehari?" I asked.

"It is a shadow cloak. It lets me blend in to my surroundings. I use it when I do not want to be noticed. I have no intention of alerting Jex until necessary. Now run along home, we will meet at the cave in the morning. Stay in bed tonight, do not be tricked into going outside or opening the windows.

While I don't think The Corruption knows who you are yet Peter I would hate to be wrong. Guide, tonight when you are safely inside ask the curator at the church to be on his guard. I would not wish Jex to establish a foothold in that building. If he builds a following..... Well best we don't think about it. When you meditate tonight open yourself to the voice you heard earlier. Any further assistance will always be welcome." With that he wrapped his cloak,around himself and walked to a dark corner of a building at the bottom of the street. At first we could easily spot him but as he drew into the shadows he became harder to pick out until I wasn't sure he was there at all.

Me and Bex walked slowly up the street, the grey light was fading and the streets were unnaturally quiet. In the somber light everything took on a mean tone, dark corners were full of menace and dark doorways leered at us as we passed. From a few streets over we heard the sound of breaking glass and a loud laugh. A bottle? A window? We didn't know but we sped up as we walked up the hill towards the pub. At the door to the pub me and Bex parted. I squeezed her hand before she pulled her hood up and took off up the hill towards the edifice of the church lurking over the town.

Inside the pub was deathly quiet. The TV in the corner was off and the bar was empty. I walked quietly in and looked about. I could hear something moving in the room behind the bar. I walked forward before the door behind me opened. I spun around to see Mum coming in. She held a paper bag bulging with rolls from the baker.

"Quiet in here tonight. Chris are you back there? I've brought some rolls to have with tea."

Dad stuck his head out from behind the partition wall. "Oh, hullo you two, I was just cleaning some glasses back here. Grab a table and I'll stick tea on."

Mum threw the bag of rolls to him and went upstairs to get changed. I sat at the table and fetched a wicker basket from the bar with sauces and a plastic vinegar shaker. I set them on the table and returned for the cutlery. Behind me the door opened. "Dad you've got a customer." I yelled without turning.

I returned to the table and set the knives and forks out for the three of us. Looking up the breath caught in my chest. At the bar stood a tall man in a white suit. He had lightly tanned skin and a swathe of stubble across his handsome face. His short hair was what my Dad called complicated. He smiled at me with impossibly white teeth. It was Jex. We hadn't met but it had to be. No one in Styxworth looked like this. I had to keep calm and hopefully I could get away with this. Keep calm and pray he wouldn't notice who I was.

"Hi. I'm looking for the main man in this bar. Surely a strapping young man such as you must be the owner." I smiled in spite of myself. He extended his hand and walked towards me. I was about to extend my hand when I heard Dads voice from the bar.

"Hi, sorry I was just cooking my tea in the back, can I help you at all?"

Jex withdrew his hand quickly and turned to face Dad. He smiled at him and walked over shaking him firmly by the hand. "Hi, you must be the Father of this young chap here, and presumably the owner of this fine establishment? I was hoping it would be busier, I always enjoy meeting new people."

"Well since the clouds have come and the ferry isn't sailing people are staying at home more. Can I get you a drink?" Dad rested his hand on the polished wood handle of the beer pump in front of him.

"That would be superb, can you recommend a good ale?" Again the warm smile shone out of his face. Dad pulled a pint off into a chunky glass and placed it on the wooden counter in front of him. "So you must be the owner, the innkeeper as it were?" Said Jex as he took a long draught from his beer. He set it on the counter and wiped the foam from his top lip.

"No sorry, I'm just the hired help. We're fairly new in town. The owner will be back tomorrow. As Dad turned his back to return some of the freshly washed glasses to the shelf I saw a look of anger cross Jex face. He finished his beer in one more gulp, tilting his head back in an inhuman fashion opening his jaw wide and pouring it in. He placed the empty glass on the counter and walked out. Dad looked up from the shelf below the bar as he heard the door open.

"He's  gone." I simply said.

"Odd chap, and see here his glass, no fingerprints, almost like he was wearing gloves. How odd. Hey ho, I better go and check on those chips. Don't want to burn tea." He pulled a funny face and returned to the kitchen. I let go,of the breath I think I'd been holding since the demon entered the bar. My shoulders sagged and I slumped back onto the bench behind the table.


The next morning I awoke early. I couldn't wait to tell Bex and Mehari about Jex visit last night. I was sure that if he had shaken my hand he would have felt the qi bubbling inside of me. After a quick breakfast I only picked at I almost ran out into street. There was no sign of Bex so I ran up the hill towards the church. A thick fog covered the streets, and the buildings once friendly and inviting seemed to leer at me. Familiar streets became abstract as objects lurched out of the slowly turning fog. As I ran up the hill towards the church the fog began to thin until I could see the steeple looming above me somehow clear of any mist. The sky above was a deep grey and large clouds hung heavy and pregnant with malice.

I knocked on the door of the small house next to the church, my small fist making next to no noise on the thick wood. The Vic answered, saw me, smiled and let me in. Bex sat at a small table in the kitchen picking at her breakfast. The dark circles under her hollow eyes attested to the lack of sleep last night.

"Morning Pete." She mumbled

"Wotcha" I said back. She smiled weakly and put the piece of toast she'd been turning over in her hand down. She picked up her plate and swept the remains of her breakfast into the bin.

The Vic stood in the door, shook his head and stood aside as we walked past him into the street.

"Geez where did the fog come from Pete? It's like a horror film out here."

"I've got a fair idea and I think it involves the man in the pub last night."

"What man?" Bex said sharply.

"Jex came into the pub when Dad was making tea last night. He wanted to speak to the owner. He was being really pally, like a game show host, friendly but false. He nearly shook my hand, then Dad came back to the bar.

As Jex spoke to him he found out Dad wasn't the owner and he drank up and left." I gabbled quickly.

"And he didn't twig that you're the Traveller?" She asked.

"He didn't seem to. But I think if he had shaken my hand he might have done. Looks like you had a rough night. More visions?"

"Not really, but I could hear shouting and arguing in the street, and at one point something howled. I don't think it was human. But whenever I think of the woman's voice speaking through me I get a feeling of comfort. Odd but I think she's kind of with us."

We walked down towards the beach avoiding the dock as much as possible. The crowd of grey people were there pushed up against the waters edge. It looked like they were swaying slightly as if held in a trance.

We reached the cave and slipped inside. The light hadn't improved much. Inside I placed a hand on the wall. Mehari sat in the middle in his usual position. He was still wearing his cloak. It seemed to absorb light making his body hard to define. He looked up as we entered.

"Good morning to you both. I hope you are both rested as today promises to be an arduous one." He looked at our drawn faces. "No matter, a little meditation before we depart. Guide, see if our female friend is looking out for us."

She nodded and dropped into a cross legged position. Her eyes closed and her breathing deepened at once.

"Did you find anything out last night?" I asked Mehari.

"Only that Jex is up to his usual tricks, setting up petty squabbles between people to destabilise the natural unity between the residents." He replied.

"He came in the pub last night looking for the owner." I told him.

"Did he now. I'm guessing he didn't see you for who you are?" He said stroking his beard.

"He didn't but I think if he had touched me he would have."

"He might have, but as I said before, Jex is not a bright being. He is too wrapped up in his own self image to notice other people properly. Now to meditation. Try to concentrate on the coming encounter. Put your mind out there, try to feel the Corruption, know his form." With that Mehari closed his eyes.

I sank into cross legged position. As I closed my eyes I breathed out, trying to clear my mind and send it out. I breathed slowly in then out again. My heart rate slowed and my mind drifted. On the next breath I felt something out there in the dark of my mind. Like a storm cloud on the horizon, a tornado below it advancing toward me. Within the tornado I sensed an eye slowly opening and closing, scanning this realm looking for me. My mind froze until I felt another presence. It was Bex, but she looked different. She was grown up, her hair had gone from mousy brown to flaming red, and her cheeks from drawn and pale to rosy red health. She pulled me back behind her and together we retreated toward a cave. Our cave. We both awoke with a start, gasping a little from the shock of coming round so quickly. Mehari opened his eyes and looked over at us both as we stared at each other.

"Was that real?" Gasped Bex.

"I think it was, I think we saw into the realm of the Corruption." I said.

Mehari stood and we followed suit. "We shall put this off no longer. The Corruption knows of you now, we will meet him and banish him back to the under realm that it inhabits.

We filed out of the cave onto the sandy beach. The thick fog swirled around us masking any sound or view of the nearby village. Bex had brought the stereo and Mehari had his cape wrapped around him. He turned to us, looked as if he was about to speak then turned and walked off up the beach. We followed briskly behind him keeping close as the thick mist pressed in on us from all sides. We didn't speak on our trek up the beach, Bex held the stereo tightly in her hands and I tried to remember the fighting positions from my qi training.

Presently we passed by the ferry dock, the grey hoard straining at the barrier to the water. At the back of the pack where there was a little more room the people were continuing to sway slightly back and forth. We passed quickly by, heads down intent on our destination. On the far side of the dock we once more walked on the beach. The deep sand slowing our progress somewhat. As we got closer to the mouth of the river the fog started to thin a little. From out of the dense mist shapes emerged like ghosts. Wooden posts and broken planks stood near the roiling water, on the other side the swelling sand dunes could be made out heaving their mass into the grey curtain of fog. Tufts of yellow grass crowned one or two of these sandy lumps. Then something I didn't expect, the sound of a guitar. Played well but not pleasantly. The chords jangled aggressively and the tone was harsh. The tune was one I felt I knew but at the same time was not familiar. It grew louder as we walked toward the ocean.

Then it stopped. The sound was cut off as a hand was laid across the strings. Into the silence a voice spoke with the sound of an old coffin being wrenched open it creaked and sputtered, several voices seemed to struggle for dominance as it sounded out the words.

"Is that you Mehari? It's been a while."

"It has not been long enough for my liking. Why do you continue to torment the worlds beyond your realm?" Mehari spoke into the fog.

From the curve of the dune a shape rose. It came toward us forming from vague shape into that of a man. He carried his guitar by the neck in one hand, reminding me of a farmer carrying a dead goose. He wore plain but faded jeans, and a black T-shirt. He was bare foot and had not a single hair on his head.

"Same old Mehari, getting older but still getting kids to do the fighting. These two must be the youngest yet." His eyes turned to me, "How old are you boy? Surely you ain't old enough to hold the power of a true Traveller?"

"And yet here he stands, who is the unfortunate body you have stolen this time?" Mehari simply said.

"This old thing?" He asked holding out his arms and examining them as if for the first time. "Just a young man who's ear I whispered in. He didn't like his life anymore so I brought him here and washed him in the river. So for now the body is mine. Better than the last one I think old man."

By my side I felt Bex shiver as she stood holding the stereo in her hands. The strangers eyes shifted about the group. "And you," he said addressing Bex "I know you. I'm sure I do. Didn't think we'd meet again. Not after last time."

Bex lifted her head and stared into his face. Cold fury flashed in her eyes. "I've never seen you before, how can you know me?"

"You don't know this body, that much is true. But we've met. I whispered into the ear of your neighbour before he attacked you. Such a shame he was so weak a man. Couldn't finish the job in hand."

Uttering a feral roar Bex dropped the stereo and ran at the man her arms wind milling. Trying to strike out, to maim, disfigure, punch, lost in her fury. The man sighed and raised his hand like a conducted stopping a train. Bex was stopped in her path like she'd hit a brick wall. She lay in the sand at his feet breathing deeply the anger burning deep inside.

"It would seem that our spirits are opposed. I can no more touch you than you touch me. That might be why you ended up here rather than fodder for your nasty neighbour. Ironic that you should meet the Traveller really." He chuckled deep in his throat.

"It's not irony if it serves deeper purpose, you of all people should know that." Said Mehari calmly. "Now, are you willing to return to your dark realm and leave these good people to cross of their own free will, or do we have to stop you?"

"Oh I think we both know the answer to that old man. You and the pup can try and stop me, but that idiot demon is running around town stirring things up. If he can get into the church on the hill I can command this realm from there. Now stand aside or be thrown into the river."

"You do know imbalance can never last." Mehari calmly said.

"But it's so much fun trying. Remember the last Traveller you brought against me? I'm not sure he really believed in himself did he."

"Regretfully I don't think he did, but you were stopped then and you will be stopped now."

Behind me Bex had pressed play and the music spilled from the speakers on the stereo.

With a sound like many people coughing together the man began to laugh. "I'm not going to battle with music again, last time it cost me a fiddle made of gold. A dance off maybe?" He continued to laugh.

I took up the first fighting position, trying hard to summon the feeling of qi building within. The man who had been doubled over laughing suddenly straightened up and threw a stiff arm out toward me. A blast of energy hit me square in the chest. I was knocked off my feet reeling from his blast of dark qi. It felt like my qi, but it felt different, a feeling of lament and sorrow passed over me and the sensation of many insects covered my skin. I clawed at my skin as the sensation burned over and through me. From far away I could hear the creature's coughing laugh start up again.

"Oh Mehari you do amuse me, a little music while I stamp on your pup. Best fun I've had in an aeon."

I slowly regained my feet as the burning stopped. "Traveller, concentrate, defend then attack." Mehari calmly spoke and Bex turned up the volume on the stereo.

I assumed my defensive stance, a familiar tingle rising up through the back of my legs let me know that I was channeling my qi again. The man shot both hands toward me like he was pushing away an attacker. The force of his blow rocked me back on my heels, the training in the cave hadn't prepared me for the full force of a qi battle. This time his dark qi didn't burn as much, I could feel it but it felt far away, as if from behind a quilt. I raised my arms to counter attack when I was hit by a second blow. Again I was knocked to off my feet. "You need to be quicker than that boy, I can see your moves coming a country mile off. What has this old fool be teaching you?"

I jumped to my feet and raised one hand while shoving my arm straight toward him. It was a good strong blast and it caught the creature on one shoulder, spinning him round. "Mehari is teaching me to defeat the likes of you." I shouted firing off a blast of qi energy that took the creature off his feet. From his prone position he pointed a finger at me. The shot felt like a hornet sting and staggered me back. "He should have told you I don't fight fair boy, I fight to win." With those words he flipped onto his feet and gave me another huge qi shove that knocked me onto my back. I writhed in pain as his dark energy coursed through my body. From no where an idea came to me. I slipped off my trainers and climbed back to my feet. I could feel the energy bubbling and fizzing through me driving out the dark qi from his last attack. He threw another at me but I was ready, assuming the defensive position. Instead of burning me, this shot crackled around me. I walked toward him while he fired off shot after shot of dark qi. Every time he hit me the energy crackled around me, my hair stood on edge and I seemed to float. I could feel a connection with the qi I hadn't felt before. It felt like I was standing above a lake ready to have the power of the entire body of water flow through me. I walked closer to him as he tried again and again to knock me back. His attacks had taken on the significance of drops of paint in a river. I reached out and grabbed his head. My hands burnt as they touched his skin and I could feel the Corruption writhing below. I locked eyes with him and behind the soulless eyes of the man I could see the creature behind him. He grabbed my wrists and tried to wrench my hands away from his face. I tightened my grip, trying to reach behind the flesh of the man to the creature below. The music from the stereo filled my ears as my mind went blank, letting the power take over me. My hands sank through the mans skull as if it didn't exist and I touched the creature within. I grabbed hold of it tightly feeling the ancient dark power of the Corruption beneath my hands. We screamed together as a vibration coursed through us. My qi and the Corruption's dark energy were meeting and trying to wrestle for control. I dug into the sand below my feet, sinking my toes into the cool sand and tightened my grip. The vibration had turned into a deep hum that was shaking us both. Forcing the man down to his knees I started tugging the creature loose from deep inside him. Our faces were inches from each other and our screams dropped in pitch to match the ethereal hum.

I felt something give way beneath my hands, I had the creature now. I stood up straight and wrenched it up and away from the shell of the man. The man's body fell face down an empty vessel like a shed snake skin. In my hands I held the essence of the Corruption, like an octopus made from smoke it churned and boiled in my grip, tentacles forming and combining, shifting and writhing. In horror I threw it out towards the river. It landed on the bank and crawled into the raging water. The humming vibration stopped. The song ended. Exhausted and spent I fell forward onto the cool sand next to the body of the man I'd removed the creature from.

I opened my eyes and looked into the dark. A soft pulsing glow let me know that we were in the cave. I felt as if I'd been locked in a washing machine on full spin. My head spun as I sat up. My body ached and burned from the ordeal. In the glow I could see Mehari sat in his meditation position. Bex was sat with her back to the wall and her head rested on her arms. I coughed and her head whipped up. "Pete, you're ok?"

"I don't know about ok, but I'm alive. Did we win?"

"Almost Peter, the idiot demon Jex is still running around town unaware you have driven the Corruption from this realm. We need to stop him before he reaches the church, but you needed a rest and a recharge. I carried you here to the cave so you could rest a while." Mehari smiled as he said this. Even in the dark of the cave I could see the twinkle in his eyes. "You performed beyond expectation Traveller, the Corruption has been sent back to the other side of the river for now. The only thing left is to send Jex after him."

Shaking my head I rose a little unsteadily to my feet. The floor of the cave was cold under my bare feet. "Did any one grab my trainers?"

"Right here Petey." Said Bex holding up my shoes. "Now let's go and kick some shiny demon butt."

We walked out of the cave onto the beach. It was late afternoon but the cloud cover and fog made it feel much later. "He will be up in the town coercing people into acts of violence and cruelty. He thrives on the chaos and will be sure to try and grab power by offering to cease the problems." Said Mehari.

Walking slowly up the beach and stretching my aching limbs I asked Mehari about the weather. "If the Corruption is gone why is it still dark and foggy here. I thought as he departed it would clear."

"It must be the doing of Jex, I didn't think he had it in him but I'm guessing the Corruption showed him how." Was all Mehari could say.

In the town the fog was at its thickest. Sounds and perspective were distorted and bent out of shape. Familiar streets pulsed with menace as strange noises came to us out of the mist. A woman screamed and was silenced, the sound flat and lifeless,and somewhere in the next street a window was smashed. We walked up the hill toward the church. We turned the corner where the pub sat, it's door was firmly closed and no light came from within. I trembled a little at the thought of my parents locked inside. Our party of three carried our walk up the hill. The baker on the next street up was also shut but his front window had been daubed with paint, a lurid slogan standing out over the gold print of his baker shop. As we climbed the hill the fog seemed to thin a little, and we could see the outline of the steeple of the church. As we drew closer we could hear shouting and yelling from nearby.

Standing outside the gateway of the church was Jex, clad in his smart white suit. He was shouting at the building, yelling at who, we couldn't see. I coughed to announce our arrival. He stopped yelling and turned to us.

"Oh if it isn't the musketeers. An old man and two kids. You can't stop me you know. I'm here, I just need to be allowed in before I can start my rule over this town."

"Why do you need to be let in?" I asked.

"If you expect to rule a land you can take it by force, but the smart solution is to take it by will. The people elect you to rule and their problems stop. With my permission to enter this church I will have the will of the people, all of the people." He snarled as he turned and rattled the gate again. "But the stupid vicar won't let me in. He seems to think his God will stop me from getting my way. He doesn't seem to realise that I control things here."

"Jex, the Corruption has been sent back across the river and we intend to send you after him." Said Mehari calmly.

"That old slug doesn't control me old man."

"He led you here and told you how to take over and this is the way you repay him? With gratitude like that I can see why you would wish to remain here."

"Of course you can, now try and join me to persuade the vicar to open these gates and let me take charge."

Mehari shook his head and stepped back. I stepped forward towards the demon and raised my fists ready to attack when I felt a hand on my shoulder. I turned to see Bex, her hand on my shoulder. She had a funny look in her eye and a Mona Lisa smile on her face. She stepped around me and stood in front of Jex. "Do your followers see you here?" She asked in a voice that came from around, beyond and through her.

"Is this an afternoon of stupid questions or what? Of course they know I'm here. The violence and problems of Styxworth will stop when I gain power. They know that. Each of them has performed  a small service in return for a solution to a problem. They want me here so they can get back to normality." He said grinning.

"Then an example must be made." Said Bex. A glow was surrounding her and she was vibrant with power. Her skin shimmered like gold and she rose into the air. Raising her hands toward the heavens the glow around her grew in intensity. She pushed her hands down and rose further into the air.

Then the fog seemed to draw up toward her. The grey blanket covering the town swirled up around her as she turned and rose further into the air. As she turned it twisted into a cloak around her draped over her glowing shoulders it pulsed silver and the train below her grew as she turned in the air. I looked around me stunned and speechless. The fog had cleared from the streets and formed into a pulsing silver dress around my friend. Everywhere I could see people with the same expression as me. I looked at Mehari and even he looked stunned.

Bex floated back toward the ground and I noticed her hair seemed to be a deep shade of red I hadn't noticed before and her cheeks were flushed with power.

"You have been played false by this demon. He no more commands the weather or deeds of good people than he controls the river." Bex spoke in a rich clear voice. "Banish him from your hearts, do not let him rule. Banish him from this land and your world will be restored with balance. These beings do not control the weather and they should not control your hearts. Make up with your neighbours and stand together against the fear and confusion this demon brings. Only then will you be free of him and his kind."

I looked around at the people that were beginning to gather around me in a crowd. As if waking from a dream I could hear them muttering their dissent at Jex. The feeling running through the crowd was turning against him and growing stronger. As more people turned up the stronger that feeling got. Jex turned to address the crowd. "I promised an end to your problems, you each did me a small service and I in turn promised you a solution. Don't believe this shiny child. I promised you."

From the crowd a stone was thrown catching Jex on the shoulder. Then another. Shielding his face with his arms he tried to yell out in protest. Every word was cut off by another stone until he was forced to turn and run from the baying crowd. Down the hill he ran chased by a hail of stones. His shouts and screams faded as he disappeared down the stony streets.

We all turned back to face Bex, intrigued to see what would be next. Without another word she raised her hands again towards the sky. She took a giant breath in and started to blow. The clouds that had been boiling and turning over the town retreated back over the river. Every where she blew the clouds were pushed back until the sky was clear. The crowd had turned to bask in the glow of the setting sun and didn't see Bex collapse to the ground after her last breath. I ran to her side with Mehari close behind. We lifted her up between us. "The cave?" I asked.

"No Pete just take me inside the church, I need some rest is all."

As the happy crowd milled around outside chatting and rejoicing we carried Bex inside, she hung limp between us as we carried her into the building.

"Is it over?" I asked Mehari.

"For now I believe it is." He simply said.

"What was that about with Bex?"

"Eos...." She gasped before she passed out on a pew.

I propped her head under a pillow and covered her with my hoodie. "What is Eos Mehari?"

"Eos is an ancient being like the Corruption, the Ancient Greeks believed her to be a Goddess who brought the dawn each morning." He said reflectively. "She must be the one who Bex has been channeling with her visions. A Guide in touch with the ancients and a powerful Traveller, well it's been sometime since that happened I must say."

A door behind us opened and the Vic appeared from it. "Is she ok? I saw what happened." He asked his voice a little shaky.

"She will be fine, she just needs to rest, channeling other beings is exhausting work. We will stay tonight to make sure Jex doesn't try to come back, but I think he's learnt a valuable lesson here today." We all laughed at this and settled in a hard wooden pew for the night.

The next morning woke us with golden light shining through stained glass, coloured pools of light fell across the seats. I awoke to see the window in front of where I had chosen to settle was St Christopher, lit from behind his image seemed to burn before my eyes.

Mehari was sitting cross legged on the floor before the altar meditating. I sat up and looked over at Bex. She was stirring and cracked one eye. I smiled at her. "Morning Bex"

"Hey Pete, are we in church?" She sat up rubbing her eyes. The Vic stirred from a few pews over.

"Yup. Apparently channeling ancient beings is quite the exhausting process!" I said smiling.

"Yeah and it gives you one hell of a head ache." She said rubbing her head.

Mehari stood and spoke to us. "I have been deep in meditation and I believe that congratulations are in order. I cannot feel the taint of the Corruption anywhere within this realm. It looks like balance has been restored."

We all grinned at each other in a silly way. "Shall we go and celebrate with breakfast at the pub?" I asked. "I want to see if Mum and Dad are ok."

"Breakfast sounds good Traveller. Lead the way."

The Vic opened the door to the church and let the early morning sunshine in. We stood on the step and breathed in the fresh air. Slowly we walked down the hill, stretching limbs aching from battle and a night sleeping in hard wooden pews. Jeff the baker was outside his shop scrubbing the paint off his window. He offered a cheery wave as our little group passed by. We reached the pub to find the door open. Mum was on the step looking nervous. She saw us coming and ran up the hill towards us. She flung her arms around me. "I'm so glad you're ok, I have been so worried. You didn't come back here last night and people were saying there had been a scene up at the church. You have no idea."

Mehari spoke "Your son and Bex here have performed a vital service restoring balance to the realm of Styxworth. Your concern is natural and we would enjoy telling you the details over some breakfast."

Mum stood and looked at Mehari, "what do you mean by a vital service?"

"Come, all shall be revealed."

"We're fine Mum, but we are all really quite hungry."

She stood aside as we all trooped into the pub. As we sat around a big table she went into the kitchen to talk to Dad. Soon a lavish breakfast had been presented and over it we took it in turns to tell my parents and the Vic about what had happened the last couple of days in Styxworth.

As we sat in our chairs around the remains of breakfast the door to the pub opened and a figure in a long black cloak came in. I jumped up but Mehari placed his hand on my shoulder, seating me again. The man looked around at us and handed Mehari an envelope before leaving with a tip of his hat.

Mehari looked at the envelope before opening it and removing the letter from within. He read from the top to the bottom before addressing us. "It would seem that Peter and Jenny are to return to the real world. You will soon awake from your coma into the everyday world. Chris I'm afraid you won't."

A deep silence descended over the table. Mehari broke it again. "Chris you can choose to stay in Styxworth or to cross over. I'm sure all the residents will be glad to have you stay."

Dad looked shocked and stared around the table slack jawed. "Uh I think I'm going to stay here and wait for Jenny to come back. When it's time we'll cross over together. I couldn't go on without her." He said.

"Very well. It shall be so." Said Mehari.

Mum sobbed and stared at Dad. They reached out and held hands across the table. I looked at Bex and saw she was crying. "I'm being selfish if I tell you I want you stay Pete, it's been great seeing you here, we've had so much fun." Cried Bex.

I felt a hitch in my throat at the thought I might not see Bex again.


With that the pub began to fade and dissolve around me. It faded to a white so bright I couldn't look at it. I screwed my eyes up. There was something lodged in my throat, I choked and coughed at the intrusion, reaching my hands up I could feel a pipe from my face and wires and tubes in my hands. I opened my eyes again and saw a hospital room full of nurses standing over me. I coughed again a clawed at the tube in my throat. I felt a soothing palm on my forehead and a voice in my ear telling me to calm down. With the light behind her red hair I thought it was Eos. Tears ran down my face as I thought of Bex left behind in Styxworth.


Pete stopped talking and looked over at the girl at the window. He had been talking for hours and she hadn't moved. She had stayed motionless at the window looking out to the street as if looking for something.

"That's quite a tale." I said to Peter. "How did you come up with it all?"

"It's no tale, it's all real, Bex show him the coin." The girl at the window turned her haunted eyes toward me and pulled a large gold coin from her pocket. She flipped it over to Pete. He handed it to me. It was a large, thick gold coin covered in oriental style writing. I turned it in my hands.

"What is it?" I asked.

"Mehari's calling card" she said.

"You went back?" I asked stunned.

"I had to, many times. The Corruption cannot be destroyed only pushed back. Every time I defeat him he gets more upset. This is my life now."

"Is that what she's watching for?" I had more questions than words at the moment.

"There are holes between the realms, I use them to return back but the Corruption is using them to try and hunt us here. He wants us dead and in his realm for revenge." Pete sighed and rubbed at his tired face.

"So what happens now?" I stuttered.

"We need to find somewhere safe to sleep. Then next time I will tell you about our trip into the realm of the Corruption."

"You crossed the river?" I stared in disbelief.

"I had to. It took my Dad."

124

The Beginning.

Printed by Amazon Italia Logistica S.r.l.
Torrazza Piemonte (TO), Italy

11490927R00073